The Pony Whisperer

Team Challenge

Collect all the Pony Whisperer books:

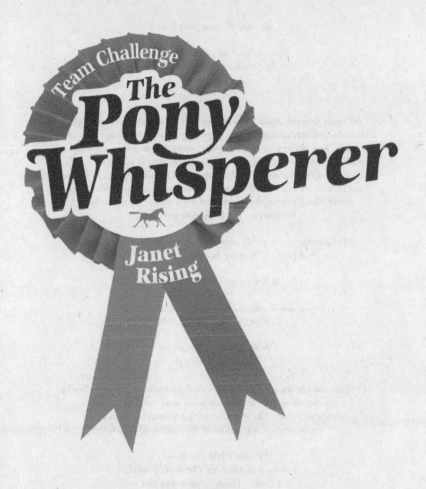

Team Challenge

The Pony Whisperer

Janet Rising

Hodder
Children's
Books

A division of Hachette Children's Books

Copyright © 2009 Janet Rising

This edition first published in 2009
by Hodder Children's Books

5

ISBN-13: 978 0 340 98842 8

Typeset in AGaramond by Avon DataSet Ltd,
Bidford on Avon, Warwickshire

Printed in Great Britain by
Clays Ltd, St Ives plc

The paper and board used in this paperback by Hodder Children's Books
are natural recyclable products made from wood grown in
sustainable forests. The manufacturing processes conform to the
environmental regulations of the country of origin.

Hodder Children's Books
a division of Hachette Children's Books
338 Euston Road, London NW1 3BH
An Hachette UK Company
www.hachette.co.uk

To my inspirational friend, Pia

Chapter One

"Hey, Pia," hissed James, sticking his head over Drummer's stable door, "lend us You-know-who for a bit, will you?"

"What's the problem?"

"I need to ask Moth why she's started to drop her hind legs over jumps, taking the poles with her. I bet it's something I'm doing wrong," James added, "it always is."

I handed James the little statue of a tiny stone woman sitting sideways on a stone horse that I *always*, always have hidden safely in my pocket. It's with me whenever I go to the stable yard where I keep Drummer. Moth is stabled next door to Drum, and no-one – but no-one – except James and me knows the secret of Epona (code name You-know-who) and we've both sworn to keep it that way!

"Thanks!" he said, and disappeared to have a chat with his pony. That's right – a bit of a chinwag. Because even though her nose is missing and she's getting on for 2000-odd years old, Epona (are you ready for this?) has the power to let whoever is holding her hear what horses and ponies are saying and be able to talk to them.

I know! When I found the ancient symbol of the Celtic and Roman goddess of horses and heard Drummer talking to me, I could hardly believe it, either. But because of Epona, and because I hadn't had the sense to keep what I discovered about the horses and ponies around me to myself, I had been proclaimed the Pony Whisperer, and all hell had broken loose. I'd helped horses and ponies who had problems, I'd upset people by telling them things they didn't want to hear, I'd even been on the telly – twice! Since then, I've tried to live it down and escape the public eye because believe me, being the Pony Whisperer may sound glamorous (I thought so too until it all got out of hand), but in reality Epona gets me into the sort of fixes I want to avoid these days.

Avoiding attention has *not* been one of my most successful ventures.

Of course, with Epona helping James I couldn't carry

on the conversation I'd been having with Drummer, but as Katy and Bean chose that moment to lean on Drummer's stable door like weird twins, it was just as well. (As Katy has red hair and is shorter than me and Bean is nothing like her they don't look anything like twins, but you get where I'm coming from.)

"Pia," announced Katy, shoving her hair off her face and puffing out her cheeks, "you and Drum have got to be in our team, haven't they Bean?"

"Yeah, yeah, you've sooo got to be," agreed Bean, beaming at me. Her real name is Charlotte Beanie, but everyone calls her Bean. With her height (tall), build (slim) and hair colour (blonde), she is the perfect match for her elegant palomino pony, Tiffany.

I was delighted they wanted to include me as I still felt very much the new girl at the yard. Everyone else there had known each other for ages, and although my Pony Whisperer title had ensured I hadn't been ignored, I didn't feel like I was really one of the gang. Drummer had been welcomed with open hooves by his fellow equines – apart from one, who I'll tell you about . . .

"We're taking the Sublime Equine Challenge," Katy announced, "and we just need you to complete our team of four."

"Yeah, we need someone to do the Wild Card," explained Bean. "Me and Tiffany are doing the show jumping – way-hey – and Katy and Bluey are our cross-country entry, natch!"

"I can't wait!" enthused Katy, "It'll be an opportunity to wear my new cross-country colours."

"What colour are they, then?" I asked, winding her up. Katy has a thing, bordering on obsession, about purple, and her last cross-country shirt and matching skull cap cover would have made a Roman emperor envious. Her new colours were reputed to be even more lairy.

When I'd first met Katy, I had been able to tell her – courtesy of Epona – that her chunky blue roan pony, Bluey, longed to go cross-country jumping. Katy was nervous, but Bluey's talent soon built her confidence. It was one of my pony-whispering successes, before things had taken a downward turn.

"Any chance of starting from the beginning?" I asked them. For an answer, Katy shoved the latest PONY Magazine under my nose and jabbed her finger on the full page ad which read:

ARE YOU READY FOR THE SUBLIME
EQUINE CHALLENGE?

Yes, I thought, I definitely am. It was the start of the

summer holidays and I was looking forward to six weeks of being with Drummer, entering some shows and going riding, especially with James, as often as I could. Did I mention that James is rather lush? No? Well, he is. The trouble is, I'm not the only one who thinks so . . .

Katy shook the magazine impatiently at me. I read on.

Sublime Equine, the new, up-to-the-minute equine wear specialists, are searching for the top all-round, junior riding team in the country.

Could that be you?

Four riders under the age of sixteen must each compete in their chosen disciplines of Show Jumping, Cross-country, Dressage and the Wild Card Event, where anything goes! After regional qualifiers, the finals will be held at the All England Jumping Course, Hickstead, at the famous British Jumping Derby meeting.

All finalists will win a complete riding outfit from the new Sublime Equine Derby range.

For full details on how to enter go to www. sublime-equine/hickstead-challenge.co.uk.

"Wow!" I said. "Drummer could do the jumping, I suppose. We're not very good at dressage or . . ."

"Not so fast!" interrupted Katy, her green eyes flashing. "Bean and Tiff are doing the show jumping – we just told you that, and I'm doing the cross-country . . ."

"Not that Tiff's brilliant at jumping, actually, but she's not bad," mumbled Bean, interrupting.

In the few months Drum and I had been at Laurel Farm DIY Livery Stables, I'd discovered that Katy was just like Bluey – positive, bouncy, enthusiastic and ready for anything. Bean, on the other hand, was away with the fairies for most of the time, which made things interesting. Although, like I said, I'm still the new girl, I'm getting to know everyone. It still gets dead awkward when Catriona turns up because she does nothing to help me feel at home and makes it clear Katy and Bean are her friends. Catriona, I should explain—

". . . and we thought you and Drummer would be fantastic at the Wild Card thingy-wotsit," Katy finished.

"Did you?" I replied, doubtfully. "What would we have to do?"

"That's just it," said Katy, waving her arms about in

her best windmill impression, "anything you like! Something whacky. Something different. You and Drum will be brilliant!"

I wasn't at all sure about that and could tell Katy was talking this Wild Card thing up. She was doing her usual '*Oh look, the glass is half-full*' thing.

"Can't we do the dressage?" I asked, doubtfully.

"Oh, yeah, if you like," said Bean, pulling her fringe down and staring at it all cross-eyed.

"Dee-Dee's doing it on Dolly Daydream, remember?" Katy sighed in exasperation at Bean before turning back to me. "With Dolly being so well schooled for the show ring, she'll be perfect. And, being a dappled grey, she looks glam, too."

I couldn't help thinking it would be pretty amazing to make up a team and get to Hickstead. I'd gone to the famous arena with my old mate Kirsten to watch the National Schools and Pony Club Championships one year (mainly because spectators got in free!). I had been terribly jealous of the winners in their Hickstead sashes, and couldn't imagine how fantastic it would be to compete there. I daydreamed about riding Drummer in the famous arena, what a wow that would be – one of my more fantastic ambitions ticked off! Plus, I'd seen some of the riding outfits the new company Sublime Equine produced, and they were pretty good. Not all stuffy, but modern and with great colours. I quite fancied myself dressed from head-to-toe in some classy garb I couldn't ordinarily afford. I supposed I could think up something for the Wild Card event, how hard could it be? Besides, I was so pleased to be included – it seemed I was becoming one of the gang.

"OK," I said, "Drum and me are up for it!" I expected to hear some comment from Drummer who was standing behind me tugging at his haynet, but then I remembered that whilst James had Epona, Drummer and I were non-communicado! It was quite peaceful, actually.

"Hurray! We've got a full team. Fantastic!" shouted Katy, punching the air. "We'd better get practising!"

"What for?" asked Bean, yawning. We both gave her a look and she gulped. "Oh yeah, the challenge. Good idea."

Their work done, Katy and Bean prised themselves off my stable door and disappeared, leaving me to carry on grooming Drummer.

Now Drummer, I have to tell you, is *so* the best pony. He's a bright bay gelding without any white on him whatsoever. I used to think he was cute and cuddly and well, you know, nice, but Epona soon let Drummer put me straight – you'll see what I mean when I get Epona back.

"Here," whispered James, leaning over the door and furtively handing me Epona. "Thanks."

The moment Epona was in my hand I heard someone humming to themselves. It was tuneless and rather horrible so I tried to block it out.

"Was it you?" I asked James.

"Was it me what?" James's dark blonde hair flopped over one eye. It's just the right side of being too long.

"You know, causing whatever Moth was doing wrong."

"Oh, yes, of course it was. She says I'm sitting back too early as we land after the jumps, and that makes her drop her hind legs on to the pole. She can't help it. I have to sort myself out as we're going in for this Sublime Equine Challenge thing."

"Are you? Who are you with?" I wished James was in our team, but remembered that we already had four team members.

"Leanne's team," said James. "Leanne is the dressage diva, of course. Cat asked me if I'd do the show jumping – which is why I need to sort myself out."

"Who's your fourth team member?" I asked. I felt

slight stirrings of annoyance that James and Cat were in the same team together and the tuneless singing in the background wasn't helping my mood.

"Dunno, Leanne's the team leader, she probably knows loads of people, she's always out competing at dressage shows," James replied, going into Moth's stable and closing the door.

I went back to picking out Drummer's hooves. "Can you whistle?" I asked him.

"What, with these lips? Of course not! Why do you ask?" Drummer replied before resuming the humming.

"Because you can't sing!" I told him.

"Oh ha, ha!" said Drummer. "And what's all this nonsense about some team you're cooking up? You lot just love thinking up new ways to make us ponies work, work, work, don't you!"

You see what I mean about Drummer? He's not exactly enthusiasm personified.

"I do hours and hours of work every day at school," I told him. "You think you're hard-done-by if you do an hour's hack."

"But then, of course, we do have to carry your huge carcasses around whilst we do it," Drummer replied smartly, twirling his haynet around with his nose because he knows it takes me ages to unravel it again.

I continued picking out mud and stones. Drummer continued to hum and sing to himself. Tunelessly. As I worked, I thought about James being in Leanne's team. Leanne does nothing but dressage on her good-looking dun pony, Mr Higgins. Poor Mr H is always rugged up, even in the summer, to keep his coat clean and lying flat, and Leanne, being a bit older than me and one of Catriona's best buddies, is not exactly my best chum. Actually, I think she's well up herself most of the time. And she's got multiple ear piercings so when the sun's out, the glare can be blinding. At least she's civil to me, which is more than can be said for Catriona.

I was going to tell you about Catriona, wasn't I?

Cat hates me.

Let's count the ways.

Cat hates me because everyone says I'm a pony whisperer, and she insists that I'm lying.

She hates me, James says, because she used to be the one everyone at the yard sought advice from until I rolled up able to tell it from the horse's mouth, so to speak.

And Cat fancies James.

And I refused to swap stables with her when I first arrived – Drummer's stable is sandwiched between Moth and Bambi, Cat's skewbald mare.

I hope you're following this 'cos it's not easy. Anyway, you get the general gist: Cat hates me; Drum's stable is between Bambi and Moth; we both rate James (but he doesn't know, I'd die if he did!). Oh, and as if that wasn't enough, Drummer fancies Bambi, and Bambi hates Drum. So now you know. And if anyone out there has ideas on how we can all live happily ever after, I'm all ears!

When I'd finished grooming Drummer, I saddled him up and as I led him out, Bean asked whether she and Tiffany could ride with us. So I said, yes, of course. It seemed I really was starting to be accepted at the yard. The drive led straight to the bridlepath and we soon passed the place where Drummer and I had found Epona; where I first heard Drummer and his take on life and my life – had changed completely.

When my mum and I had moved to this area, after my mum and dad's marriage broke down, we had known it was rich with history. There had been Roman settlements in the area two thousand years ago (hence Epona), and as the highest point for miles around, it had been a popular place for building through the centuries. Laurel Farm used to belong to the big house, long since gone. And I mean big, I'm talking servants, carriages and everything.

With Epona in my pocket, I could hear Drummer and Tiffany chatting. Drummer's bright mahogany neck and black mane contrasted strongly against Tiffany's snowy-white mane and golden palomino coat as their heads bobbed in unison.

"What's this about some competition, this Hickstead thing?" asked Drum.

"Oh that!" replied Tiffany. "Sounds worrying. Still, if it wasn't that, it would be something else. Oh, what's that?" Tiffany put in an abrupt stop, waggled her ears and then walked on again. (She's like that, always on the lookout for anything a bit suspect. On a bad day she goes along like one of those balls fixed by elastic to its own bat; forward-back, forward-back, forward-back. Bean's used to it and just ignores her. They're completely unalike – Tiff's all *Whaaa!* while Bean's so laid-back, she's practically *zzzzz-ing* all the time.)

"Get a grip," sighed Drummer, "it's just a crisp packet."

"Oh so it is. Phew. You never know . . ."

"Never know what? When a crisp packet might turn nasty?" asked Drum. He's not exactly sympathetic to Tiff's nerves.

"You just never know, that's all. If my ancestors hadn't had their wits about them, I wouldn't be here now."

"So what's your role in the Hickstead malarky?"

"What? Oh, that. Er, let me think. Oh I remember, show jumping. I hope they won't expect me to slide down that Derby bank. No thank you, I don't do heights!" Tiffany sniffed. "What's your speciality?"

"No-one's told me yet!" said Drummer.

It didn't sound like the ponies were exactly bursting with enthusiasm. When we got back to the yard, Katy and Dee-Dee were both outside Dolly's stable wearing identical, thunderous expressions. Dolly nickered to Drummer when we got near. Dee's beautiful dappled grey show pony has a bit of a thing for Drummer.

"What's up with you two?" asked Bean. "You look like you want to murder someone."

"Yes, well, you will too when you hear," said Katy, grimly.

"Tell us then," I said, jumping off Drummer and running my stirrups up the leathers.

"Dee's mum won't let Dee enter Dolly for the dressage."

Bombshell!

"What? Why not?" exploded Bean.

"Oh well, get this," Dee whined, "she says we've got too many top shows to go to. Says it will ruin Dolly's chances. Says she's hoping we'll qualify for the Horse of the Year Show this year."

"But . . ." began Bean.

"No buts!" interrupted Katy, doing an uncanny impersonation of Dee's mum and sticking her hand up, palm towards us. "Subject closed!"

"Crikey, Dee," I said, "can't you do something?"

Dee rolled her eyes. "What do you think? It's all right for you, your mum isn't horsey. You know how much I hate being dragged off to shows every weekend, I'd rather be having fun with all of you. My mum's made it clear that while she's paying the bills, she'll have the last say. I never get to have any fun on Dolly; I just wish she was an ordinary pony, like all of yours."

"Excuse me?" cried Katy, her hackles rising.

"Oh, you know what I mean!" moaned Dee, lost in self-pity.

I sucked in my cheeks. Dee's mum Sophie is a showing fanatic and used to getting her own way. She has her own show horse, a liver chestnut called Lester (with some fancy show name) and their lorry is probably bigger than the house I live in with my mum. And Sophie is the sort of horsey woman who won't take no for an answer. Poo! I was getting quite excited about this competition. Now we seemed to have failed before we'd even begun.

"You're let off, then," I heard Drummer say to Dolly.

"Yes," Dolly sighed. "And I was so looking forward to spending more time with you, handsome," she added, batting her eyelashes at my bay pony.

I told you, didn't I?

"Maybe we'll all get out of it," Tiffany sounded hopeful.

"Bet we're not that lucky!" Drummer groaned.

"But what about me? What am I supposed to do all summer?" moaned Dee, picking flaking green paint off Dolly's door with her fingernail.

"Don't worry about that," Katy said brightly, smiling at Dee. "When you're not qualifying for HOYS you can be the team groom."

"Oh big deal!" exclaimed Dee, flicking her brown hair and storming off in a huff to the barn.

"How about James?" Katy suggested. "He might be on our team."

"Cat and Leanne have already bagged him," I said.

"We have to find someone," Bean wailed, jumping off Tiffany. Tiff woke up with a start, suddenly alert to any tigers or crocodiles or wolf packs which could be lurking – like they do around an English stable yard.

"We will!" I said grimly. "We just have to!"

Chapter Two

Despite our depleted team, we began to practise for the Sublime Equine Challenge. At least, Katy and Bean did. I just sat about wondering what on earth Drummer and I could do for the Wild Card event. What would the judges be expecting? I couldn't get my head round it – whatever could we do that was different and exciting? I couldn't let Katy and Bean down.

I explained the concept to Drummer.

"Why can't we just do the show jumping?" he said.

"Because Bean and Tiff have bagsied that."

"Well, ask if we can do the cross-country. I can do that – if I have to."

"Bluey's doing it. He'll die of disappointment if anyone else does it and he's way, way better at it than anyone else."

"Well, I could just about manage the dressage, I

suppose," said Drum in his best martyr voice.

Of course! Now Dee was out, perhaps Drum and I could nick the dressage slot. I thought hard. Dressage isn't our best thing, really. To be honest, we're not great at anything in particular, but we are sort of passable at everything – you know, we get by and win the odd rosette. We'd probably do a better dressage test than a pathetic Wild Card routine, though.

I found Bean in the outdoor school, putting Tiffany over a few jumps. Katy was doing the groom bit – charging around and changing the height of the poles. She was a bit red in the face, which clashed with her red hair. The effect was sort of a raspberry topped with grated carrot. I didn't think she'd thank me for telling her that though, so I kept it to myself.

"Me and Drum really want to do the dressage," I shouted from the gate. I decided it would be better to be positive about the dressage, rather than negative about the Wild Card event. To be honest, I didn't fancy my chances much in either. Katy stopped in mid-stride and frowned.

"Oh, OK. We just need a Wild Card person now," she said. "Oi, Bean, you almost ran me over!"

"Well, you're in the way!" wailed Bean, hurtling toward the next jump, her long blonde plait flying out behind her like a tail. I couldn't help noticing Tiffany's peculiar jumping style: between jumps she cantered around all collected, looking every inch the show jumper. Then, three strides away from the jump, she stuck her head in the air, launched herself like a rocket and took off almost straight up. On landing, she resumed her rocking horse canter and melt-in-the-mouth expression. Weird!

I could hear her muttering to herself as she did it – "Oh, there's the jump . . . OK . . . here we go . . . it's a big one . . . I CAN DO IT! . . . oh, no I can't . . . maybe . . . yikes . . . YES!!!"

"How do you stay on when she does that?" I asked.

"Does what?" asked Bean airily, as Tiffany did her rocket-launch impersonation over the planks with a grunt. I supposed Bean was used to it.

I went and told Drummer the good news. He was dozing with his head in the far corner of his stable.

"So we're doing the tip-tuppy thing, now?" he said, not bothering to turn around.

"If the tip-tuppy thing is Drummer-speak for dressage, then yes," I told him.

"Oh good, I can sleep through that," he said, yawning. "I don't suppose . . ."

"What?"

". . . there's an eating category? I'm sure to win that."

"You're right there, fatso!" I told him. "In fact, I think I need to cut down your grazing hours. I may keep you in at nights for a while until the grass dies down a bit."

"WHAT?" yelled Drummer, swinging round to face me. "Are you JOKING? I eat hardly anything. I barely manage to scrounge enough out there in the field at night by the time Tiffany and that pig Henry have lawn-mowered their way around. It's a wonder I've not been reported to one of the horsey charities, I'm so starved."

Henry is a hefty, argy-bargy Dales pony who belongs to an ancient old dear called Mrs Bradley. I could well believe he was a bit of a gutso, but Tiffany never carries any weight – she and Bean are both identical in the skinny department. I decided to move the conversation on.

"We need a final team member, so put your thinking cap on."

"James and Moth," said Drummer.

"Oh, why didn't I think of that?" I said, sarcastically. "Oh wait a minute, I know, because he's been commandeered by Cat and Leanne!"

"Pippin?" Drum asked, doubtfully. I gave him a

look. Pippin is tiny and his rider, Bethany, is just a tot.

"In that case," Drum sighed, "I can't think of anyone. Can Bluey do two events? He's always got energy to spare. He makes me tired just looking at him. Talking of which, you've interrupted my nap."

Drum is so maddening at times! I decided to turn him out in the field and go home.

When I told my mum about the Sublime Equine Challenge, she thought it was a great idea.

"Oooh, imagine if you qualify for the finals," she enthused, her blonde hair bobbing in excitement, "and you get to ride at Hickstead. How thrilling would that be?"

"Well, unless we find our fourth team member, that's never going to happen," I replied. We were munching our way through an Indian takeaway, plates on our laps, watching the telly. Tin foil cartons littered the side table.

"I've got a new date tomorrow," announced Mum. My heart sank. We moved here to this cottage when my mum and dad split up. Dad went off with some size double zero chick from work, and Mum went a bit to pieces. But since we've been here she's brightened up and she's been looking for love, as they say.

On the internet.

I know, I know, it freaks me out, but what can I do? She's really careful and sensible about it, and I've promised to support her. Her friend Carol supports her too, which isn't surprising seeing that Carol dates men like we're all on a downward slide towards the end of the world. I blame Carol and her interfering ways for getting Mum into it all.

"That's nice," I said, managing to make it sound as though I meant it. I'm getting better at that. "Who's this one, then? Old or new?"

"Second date," mumbled Mum, stuffing half a samosa in her mouth and leaving filo pastry crumbs on the side of her face.

"Well, if you're going for a curry, don't do that," I advised, "it's most unattractive. Who's this one, then?"

"His name's Brian. He's a teacher. Divorced. He's got two sons, seven and twelve years old. They live with their mother. He's very nice and he was very attentive on our first date – and very interested to hear about your passion for horses. Apparently, he used to ride in his youth."

"Oh good, perhaps he can come and be our fourth team member," I suggested, glumly. "Do you think he can possibly pass as under sixteen?"

"Doubtful – he's got a beard."

"Oh yuk!"

I was getting fed up with trying to think of someone to complete our team. It was so frustrating! If only my old mate Kirsten didn't live so far away, she'd have thought up something brilliant for the Wild Card event.

The next day, I was tacking Drummer up to go for a hack by ourselves when James turned up.

"Going riding?" he said.

I nodded.

"Want some company?" he asked. "I'm a bit fed up at the moment."

Naturally, I didn't say no.

It didn't take him long to get Moth in from the field and tack up, and we rode out along the bridlepath which led down to the lake. Moth's bright chestnut coat gleamed in the sunlight, her four white legs moving in step with Drum's black ones. Moth has a white face, too, but you can't see that very well when you're riding next to her, and she always goes along in a hurry, puffing and slamming her hooves down like an old fashioned charger, with James playing the role of her knight. At least, that's how I see it.

"How's the jumping going?" I asked James. "Did your chat with Moth help?"

"Yes it did, but it's all been for nothing," James moaned.

"Why?"

"Cat told me yesterday that I can't be in her team. It appears that Leanne had already asked two of her much-more-talented-than-me friends to do the show jumping and the cross-country."

"What?" I cried, my heart leaping.

"Yeah, I know. What a bummer, eh?" continued James. "I mean, talk about a let down. She's nabbed India Hammond for the show jumping, so I'm ditched. Leanne thinks she stands a better chance with India and her brilliant pony the Dweeb, than with Moth and me. How rude!"

"But that's wonderful!" I shrieked, sitting up and reining in Drummer. I blessed India, whoever she was – selfish of me, but hey-ho.

"Oow!" said Drummer. "Tone it down, will you? Some of us have big ears."

"Thanks, you're a pal!" James exclaimed, turning in the saddle to frown at me.

"We're looking for someone to be on OUR team!" I shouted, bouncing up and down on Drum.

"Oi, I'm not a trampoline. Sit still up there or get off!" grumbled Drum.

"But . . . but . . . you've got four people already," James said.

"Not any more! Dee's mum's forbidden her to do it – says it'll ruin Dolly's chances of qualifying for HOYS."

"Oh, brilliant!" James said, beaming from ear to ear before forcing his face into looking seriously sad. "Bad luck about poor Dee-Dee, though."

"Of course."

"Yeah, of course."

I don't think either of us really meant it. Dee's a bit of a moaner. Well, actually, she never stops moaning. I suppose it's hard for her with her mum always at the stables and on her case the whole time, but even so, it's a bit wearing.

We rode on with James in a much-improved mood.

"Got our fourth team member, then?" said Drum.

"Yup!" I told him, patting his neck.

"So we're still doing it?"

"Yup!"

Drummer sighed. Moth said nothing. She's not very talkative due to her (understandable) mistrust of humans. She was mistreated before James got her, and she'll only talk to James. Of course, he can only hear her when he has Epona. We've tried holding Epona between us so we can both hear the ponies but it seems she's not a sharing sort of girl, and only works for one person at a time.

"What's Drummer's problem?" James asked, hearing me talking to him. James has known about Epona ever since he got hold of her by mistake but he'd never tell anyone else. I mean, imagine the fuss – everyone would want Epona, and I'd probably have to give her up and Drummer says that ponies everywhere wouldn't thank us. So that's why we keep her to ourselves.

"Oh, nothing important." I told him. "Let's have a canter – I'll race you!"

Katy and Bean were ecstatic when we told them.

"Fantastic!" Katy screamed, throwing her purple dandy brush in the air. Unfortunately, it landed on the roof with a bang, which made Tiffany, who'd been dozing in her stable next door, almost fall over.

"But wait a minute . . ." started Bean ". . . who's going to do which event?"

We all looked at Bean. I don't think anyone quite believed she had beaten us all to highlighting the problem.

"What?" she said. "It's an obvious question!"

"Well," I said, "we need someone to do the Wild Card." I really didn't want to get lumbered with

26

that again – I'd only just wriggled out of it.

"Er, don't think so!" said James, firmly.

"Well what, then?" said Katy, her hands on her hips. "I mean, I really, *really* want to do the cross-country."

We all agreed that Bluey was the best pony for the job.

"Moth can only do gymkhana and jumping," James said.

"But I'm doing the show jumping!" wailed Bean. "I've been practising!"

"So have I," James said. Moth only ever storms around with her nose on her chest, snorting like a dragon. She clearly couldn't do the dressage – she'd be useless at it. She had to do the show jumping.

"But Tiff's quite well schooled, isn't she Bean?" said Katy, determined to win Bean around. "She could do the dressage – Moth can't."

"I suppose so," Bean agreed reluctantly, biting her lip. "But I'm pants at remembering dressage tests. I went in for one ages ago and totally forgot the way. It was awful."

I could quite imagine Bean forgetting a dressage test.

"Oh you'll be fine!" James said breezily.

"But I'm doing the dressage!" I told them. I didn't like where this was going.

27

"You're welcome to it!" shrugged Bean. "I'll be just as useless at the Wild Card as I will be at dressage!"

"You'll be fine!" repeated James. "It's settled!"

"I didn't know it was up to you – you've swiped the show jumping, and I've been practising. Dressage isn't my thing, it really isn't!"

"Stop being so bossy, James," said Katy, firmly. "You've only been in the team five minutes and you're taking charge. It's our team, not yours!"

"I don't know why you're making such a fuss," began James, oblivious to Bean's feelings. I didn't understand why I couldn't do the wretched dressage – I wanted to, for goodness' sake, which is what I told everyone.

"But we need you to do the Wild Card event," insisted Katy.

"Why?" I said.

"Yes, why?" wailed Bean. "Tiff and I can do it. I'd rather do that than the dressage. Believe me, you really don't want me doing the dressage."

"Pia has a huge advantage – she can talk to Drum and get him to do things none of us could do with our ponies. Don't you see?" said Katy, getting all earnest in an obvious attempt to win us over. "Pia is the natural choice for the Wild Card – she has to do it!"

There was silence. That I might be a natural choice

was news to everyone but we could see how Katy was thinking. The image of Drum and me doing the dressage faded away. It seemed Bean and I were both stuck with our respective events, however much we didn't want them.

I frowned. "What do you mean, Katy? Explain."

"You just have to think up something. Some sort of routine you can talk Drummer through, something that doesn't rely on riding or tack. You could, er, well, you could . . . Oh, I don't know, how about something without any tack on at all? Wouldn't that wow the judges? You'd win by miles!"

"Yes, Pia!" exclaimed James. "That would be brilliant!"

I wasn't convinced. "Wouldn't that be cheating?"

"Why?" asked James, totally getting on board with the idea. "You need to use the skills you have. Not everyone knows you're a pony whisperer."

"It sounds like cheating to me."

"No, you're just pressing home your natural advantage," Katy continued. "Just as Leanne is really good at dressage – she's not going to take on the jumping because she thinks she has an unfair advantage in the dressage event, is she?"

When it was put it like that, it sort of made sense.

"Does that mean I'm stuck with the dressage, then?" mumbled Bean.

We all looked at her in sympathy. Katy put her arm around Bean's shoulders.

"You and Tiff can do it! Tiffany goes really well, I don't know why you don't enter for more dressage competitions, you'll be great at it."

"Because I can't remember the tests!" Bean said, through gritted teeth.

"One of us can call for you," said James. You can have someone call out the movements if you want to.

"Yes, that would work!" said Katy, squeezing Bean's shoulders.

"That's worse," said Bean, shaking her head. "It confuses me even more." She gave a big sigh. "I suppose I can give it a try," she said. "For the team."

"We'll help you learn your test," I said, impressed by Bean's attitude. I could see her being great at dressage – Katy was right, Tiffany was well schooled and Bean rode really well. I was, however, really annoyed about being forced into the Wild Card thing. My attitude sucked.

"Atta girl!" James grinned at Bean.

"You're a star!" said Katy. "Besides, only the three highest scores count, so stop worrying."

"Is that supposed to make me feel better?" said Bean, getting indignant. "I'm just there to make up the numbers, am I?"

"I just thought it would take the pressure off a bit," said Katy, going red. Bean just sighed.

It was settled at last.

I still couldn't help thinking how great it was to be in the team. Shame my event was a pile of poo!

Chapter Three

"So you're in Katy's team now?" I heard Catriona's voice. She and James were outside Moth's stable.

"That's right," I heard James reply, good-naturedly. "And we're going to thrash your team into the ground so don't get your hopes up!"

Catriona laughed and told James he had no chance.

I walked over to get Drummer's headcollar which was hanging on his door. I always dread seeing Cat; she never misses an opportunity to have a pop at me. I hate the way I feel intimidated just by her being there. Irksome!

"Oh there you are Brighton, we were just talking about you!" she smirked. Like I couldn't hear! I pulled my mouth into a fixed smile. Catriona is annoyingly pretty, with short dark hair and elfin features, and when she's not cutting me dead, she thinks it's

32

hysterical to call me Brighton instead of Pia. Get it? Yeah, I know, screamingly funny – not! The other annoying thing is that she fancies James, and as James hangs around with one of Cat's three brothers, I can't help feeling she has the drop on me. Soooo annoying!

I took myself off to bring Drummer in from the field. He was hanging around the gate, waiting for me.

"Come on, hand over that carrot!" he hissed, edging his way carefully around Cat's skewbald mare, Bambi. Bambi put her ears back and snaked her head at him. She can't stand Drummer, and he, for some unknown reason, fancies her like mad.

I thought about Catriona. I bet she was furious that James was in our team – having him in hers had been a definite coup. I grinned to myself. Too bad, Leanne didn't want him so that's their loss.

I still hadn't thought of a thing to do for our Wild Card routine. I'd gone on to www.sublime-equine/hickstead-challenge.co.uk and printed out the rules and regs. It was quite complicated. Apparently, to get through to the Hickstead final each team had to finish in one of the first three places of a local qualifier round – twice. And to make it more interesting, teams weren't allowed to enter more than three qualifiers. Tricky. And Katy was right, the highest three scores from each team counted towards the final score, with the lowest score being dropped from the total. Then I had searched for information on the Wild Card event. "*The judges will be looking for a performance from an individual which demonstrates a unique partnership with, and understanding of, their pony,*" it said.

Crikey! It didn't say whether I had to ride or whether I could be on foot. It did say each show was not to exceed four minutes duration. It didn't inspire me. No Ding! moment occurred, no mother of an idea popped into my head.

I took Drummer for a ride to see whether I could get my head round it all. Drummer took advantage of my lack of concentration and put in a couple of bucks, landing me on his neck.

"You're so not funny!" I told him.

"Oh, but I so am!" he smirked.

We turned into the woods where it was cool and damp. Through the trees I could see the sun sparkling on the lake and Drummer's hoofbeats became silent on the carpet of pine needles. I'd never been in this part of the woods before but I knew I couldn't get lost if I kept the lake in sight. I was still exploring the countryside near the stables, and finding new paths every time we went riding.

Suddenly, all thoughts of the Wild Card disappeared as Drummer slammed on the brakes and snorted, lifting his head and holding himself stiffly to attention.

"What is it?" I whispered, my hand on his neck.

"Don't know," he said. "But the ground round here feels a bit funny."

"Funny?"

"Yes. I can't explain it. There's something strange over there behind the bushes. The whole area's giving me the creeps."

I felt the hairs on the back of my neck stand up and my imagination ran riot. "Should we be getting out of here?" I whispered.

"What? No, no, it's old vibes I'm picking up. Let's take a look," Drum said, walking forward again. I didn't know whether I wanted to take a look. What old vibes? What if they were dead body sort of old vibes? And how old? It was uncanny how Drum could feel stuff.

It wasn't a dead body. We pushed our way through the bushes and there was what looked like a grassy mound with a door in it. A very old, arched wooden door, with rusty nails and a rusty handle. It couldn't be a house, unless the house was either very small or underground.

"Whatever is that?" I said.

"You're asking me?" said Drummer. "Get off and take a closer look."

I slipped out of Drummer's saddle. "Hey," I told him, "no running off and leaving me here. Promise!"

"OK, OK. You spoil all my fun."

The door was old and mossy and the handle was riddled with rust. I tried but I couldn't make it budge. Secretly, I was quite glad. I mounted Drum again.

"You are so feeble," he yawned.

"Yeah, well, I'd like to see you do any better with your hooves!" I told him, turning for home.

When we got back to the yard, Catriona had gone riding with Leanne but luckily, James was still around.

"I've just found something very strange in the woods by the lake . . ." I began.

James held up his hand to stop me. "Grassy hill with a door in it? Looks like a Hobbit house?"

"Yes!" I cried. "That's exactly what it looks like. It's not a Hobbit house, is it?"

"No, it's an old ice house," James replied. "When the big house was here, centuries ago, the people stored ice they got from the lake in the winter to use in the summer, the ice house being built into the ground stayed cold, and the ice stayed frozen for months."

"Wow! I couldn't open the door."

"Oh, I've been in it. It falls away to a huge, dark hole and you can't see the bottom of it. It's dead good!"

It didn't sound dead good. I was glad the door hadn't yielded.

"How come you know about it?"

"Most of us at the yard do – but I think we're the only ones, being as we ride around there. No-one seems to care about it. If the council knew it was there I expect they'd think it was dangerous and probably board it up or fill it in."

"Are there any other ancient buildings or strange things around here that I should know about?" I asked him: (I was intrigued by the ice house. It was dead spooky. I imagined servants cutting blocks of ice from the frozen lake, loading it on to wagons and packing it into the ice house. How cool was that? Oh, actually, that's quite funny. I'll have to remember that one.)

"Oh probably," said James. "This yard was the farmyard for the same house. The work horses would have been stabled here. The riding and carriage horses would have lived at the coach house."

"Oh, where's that? Can you show me?" I thought an old coach house sounded wonderful. I loved the way the surrounding countryside held such historic secrets.

"No. It's gone. No-one can see it. The land . . ." James paused dramatically, ". . . has reclaimed it."

I had other matters of concern.

"I can't imagine what I can do for this Wild Card event," I moaned. James threw Moth's old water away on the grass behind her stable and sat on the upturned bucket.

"Well, let's think of something. What can you do that no-one else can?"

"Nothing," I replied, miserably, flopping down next to him. "And I'm hopeless at thinking things up. Do you have any ideas?"

"Well . . . something did occur to me. You could do something like the dog show people do," mused James.

"What – agility? I can't see Drummer galloping through a cloth tunnel or weaving in and out of poles."

"No, not agility. What do they call it? Doggie dancing. You know, they put a routine together with music. You and Drum could do that. It would be different."

I thought hard. I'd seen people dancing with their dogs on the television. It looked quite fun. I could make us both costumes. We could have music. I'd always fancied myself in showbiz.

"That might work . . ." I began, "but I'd need a

theme, and music." I felt quite excited and my spirits lifted a bit. But then they plummeted again. I'd forgotten one thing – the most important thing; I was going to have to sell it to Drummer. I decided I'd defer that until I'd got a bit further with the routine idea. No need to get Drum into doubly negative mode just yet. I'd wait until I had it all planned out in my head.

The next day, at breakfast, I had to suffer the account of Mum's date with the latest man in her life.

"What a nice man!" Mum said, struggling to open a carton of orange juice.

I took a deep breath – I'd heard that before. Most of Mum's dates start off that way. By the fourth or fifth date, they begin to show their true colours and words like *nice* are replaced with *weirdo*, *lech* and *creep*. I always looked forward to the novelty wearing off.

"He was charming and very funny. I think you're going to like him, Pia."

"It sounds as though you do," I said, tucking into some toast and jam. "Mum, can I talk to you about this Sublime Equine Challenge?"

"Of course. I was telling Brian about that last night . . ."

"I've decided to do a dance-type routine with Drummer, you know, like they do with the dogs at dog shows."

"That sounds tricky. Are you sure you can do that?"

"Yes, I'm certain – I can talk Drummer through it. (*Mum knows I can talk to horses, but she doesn't know how*). But anyway, the thing is I'm going to need an outfit – and so is Drum. Do you think you can help me?"

"I'll try. I used to make your outfits for school plays, do you remember? You looked lovely in that angel's outfit I made for the nativity."

Uh-oh, nativity flashback! I'd been six years old, there had been about fifteen angels and Zoe Braithwaite was the most glamorous with huge, sparkly wings like a fairy queen. Mine were made out of wire coat hangers and my dress had been an old nightdress. I wondered whether asking Mum for help in the wardrobe department was a good idea. It was too late to backtrack now.

"What are you going to be?" asked Mum. "I've got lots of curtains from our old house in the attic, so if you can think up costumes with a floral theme, that would be handy. Did you see the rose Brian bought me at dinner? He's very romantic."

I couldn't stop my head filling up with images of Zoe Braithwaite. She had looked so glamorous. By comparison, I had looked like a clown, a jester to her queen. A jester . . . maybe there was some mileage in that idea. Maybe . . .

"What do you think about Drummer and me being a jester and a queen?" I mumbled, still working the idea around in my head. Drum could wear bells; I could get dressed up like a medieval queen, all flowing wimple and long dress. It might work . . .

"Or you could both be jesters," added Mum. "Brian's funny, too, amazing sense of humour . . ."

"Mmmm, we could." My toast had gone cold and so had my enthusiasm for Brian. He sounded a right creep to me. "I need to think about this," I told Mum. Grabbing my bag – and Epona, of course – I cycled to the yard with the queen and jester idea whirling around in my head. It could work. Frankly, I thought, it had to work because time was ticking on and we had only a week to sort out a routine and get our outfits made before the first local qualifier.

James and Katy thought it was a great idea.

"Brilliant!" enthused Katy.

"I can just see you in medieval outfits!" said James. "Bells are a genius idea."

"I don't get it," said Bean. "What exactly are you going to do?"

"Well I'm not completely sure yet," I told her. "It's

41

just an idea. It needs work."

"We'll help you work out a routine," offered Katy. "It'll be easy! Drummer will look so cute in a jester outfit with bells on – he'll love it!"

Mmmm, I thought to myself with a sinking heart. I still hadn't told Drummer – and loving it wasn't exactly how I imagined he would feel.

Chapter Four

"Let me get this straight," Drummer said. "You expect me to do that ridiculous dance routine thing – *with bells on* – in front of all these other ponies? Dream on!"

We had arrived at South Bassett Farm, where the first of the local qualifiers for the Sublime Equine Challenge was being held. James, Katy, Bean and I had all hacked over – it had only taken an hour but had seemed a lot longer because Bean was trying to remember her dressage test and we were fed up with hearing it – and now we'd arrived we were feeling less than confident. South Bassett Farm was where the local riding club held its shows and events. They had a cross-country course in the adjoining woods and the Sublime Equine team had moved in with all the paraphernalia needed to put on a show. Everyone's parents had been more than supportive about our bid for fame at Hickstead, but for various reasons couldn't make it to this, our first qualifier. I was relieved – it meant slightly less pressure on us all.

"Oh my," breathed Bean, "look at that lot!"

We followed her gaze to a team of four matching chestnut ponies. Their riders were all kitted out in identical riding clothes with blue shirts and pale ties, and the ponies all wore blue and pale blue browbands. Their blue saddle cloths had the words *Team Diamond* emblazoned across them.

"Blimey!" exclaimed James.

"Oh, I wish we'd thought of that!" cried Katy. "My mum would have made us some saddle cloths. We'll have to have some for the next qualifier."

"We'll have to choose a name, first," I pointed out. I didn't like the look of this – there were loads of teams and they all looked much more polished and confident than us. I spotted Bambi and Mr Higgins tied to Leanne's trailer; Cat and Leanne were grooming them. Their matching red polo shirts had *Team SLIC* on the back of them.

"Team names seem to be the thing," I said, wondering what SLIC stood for, and whether they'd forgotten to add the K at the end. Or maybe the letters were too big and they'd run out of space. "We totally need to think up a name for our team. We're just a number at the moment."

"How about Team Tremendous?" suggested James.

"Or Team Bossy Boy," mumbled Bean.

"Oh, good idea, Bean – you could all be James' Angels, like Charlie's!" James laughed.

"Is that supposed to be funny?" I said.

"Where's the cross-country course?" Bluey said, chomping at the bit. "I can't wait to get going!"

Tiffany was looking around the showground. "Is that just a paper bag or something worse? What's that droning noise? I hope no-one pops a balloon, and I hope my test is *soon* so I get it over with," I heard her muttering.

Moth kept her thoughts to herself as usual, and Drummer was sulking. Which was better than going on and ON about how much he didn't want to do the Wild Card.

Breaking it to him hadn't been as bad as I'd imagined – until I'd mentioned my idea for outfits.

"You expect me to wear some fancy dress get-up?" he'd asked, his ears twitching backwards and forwards.

"Yes, well, the routine depends heavily on the visual aspect," I'd explained.

"With bells, you say?" More ear twitching.

"Well, yes. Jesters wore bells."

"And you're NOT wearing bells, have I got that bit right?" He'd stared at me.

"Mmm, yes. You see, I'm the queen; a jester entertains the queen. He makes her laugh."

"I'm a figure of fun? A clown? You're glamorous and I'm the stupid one?" Ballistic ear action.

"It's only for four minutes," I'd mumbled, aware that Drummer wasn't buying into it.

"Four minutes . . ." he'd mused. "What's in it for me?"

"Excuse me?"

"What do I get out of it? What's *my* motivation?"

"Er . . . well . . . you get the satisfaction of doing your bit for the team. It's a team effort and you'll be supporting Moth and Bluey and Tiffany." I had felt quite pleased at thinking that up.

"OK, I get all that," Drum had said, dismissively, "but I'm talking about me. What do *I* get if I do this . . . this . . . pointless fancy dress parade – with bells?"

"What do you want?"

"To stay out at night. No more talk of me staying in and going on a diet."

I had thought long and hard. The grass was going off a bit now so it would probably be all right.

"Deal!"

But when I'd tried his outfit on him, Drummer had protested all over again.

"What's this stupid hat thing?" he'd said when I'd put the ear caps on him. They were proper knitted ear protectors, worn by show jumpers to keep out noise and flies. I'd managed to find some red ones at the tack shop, and Mum had sewn some yellow diamonds on to them. We'd decided that Drum's bay coat would look good in a red-and-yellow jester outfit, with a diamond pattern and bells sewn in strategic places. I'd bandaged each of Drummer's legs – two red bandages, two yellow; weaved some red and yellow ribbons in Drummer's mane and tail; and decorated a yellow headcollar with tiny red felt diamonds. With jingling budgie bells from the pet shop sewn on to the tips of the ear protectors and each leg bandage, Drum ting-a-ling-ed whenever he moved. I had been very proud of my efforts, and thought Drum looked the part without going over the top.

Drum hadn't agreed.

"So what are you going to wear?" he'd asked me, shaking his head. The bells had given a satisfactory ting-a-ling.

"I've got a wimple . . ."

"A what?"

"It's a pointy hat with a chiffon scarf tied at the top . . ."

"Like a witch?"

"Oh, if you like," I had sighed, worn out by Drum's negativity, "and a floaty yellow dress thing to wear over my jodhpurs. It's really you they'll be looking at."

"Why doesn't that make me feel any better?" Drum had grumbled.

We hadn't had many days to practise. We agreed that we'd keep it simple – that I'd stand in the middle and Drum would circle around me and turn and dance a bit, looking like he was making me laugh. Then we'd do a circuit in step together like we were dancing; throw in a few sideways moves and some back steps; and end in front of the judges and bow – with Drum putting his front hooves out in front and bending down all cute for the *ahhh* factor. It seemed to work pretty well once Drummer had mastered the bow, and I was secretly confident that we'd be fine with me telling Drum what to do and where to go.

But now we were here at the showground and the tiny bit of co-operation I'd had from Drum seemed to be evaporating. I only hoped he would see it through OK.

The field was buzzing with activity. In one corner was the dressage arena set out with white markers and the judge's car at one end. Flags announced the start of the cross-country course on the other side, and show jumps gleamed in yet another part. Horseboxes were lining up in the adjacent field, and a big secretary's tent was surrounded by promotional banners for Sublime Equine, all in their familiar orange and lime colours. Glamorous girls in Sublime Equine outfits handed out Sublime Equine catalogues. We found a shady tree to claim as our own and Katy and Bean went off to confirm our entry.

"Everyone looks alarmingly competent," said James, eyeing up one of the Sublime Equine promotional girls who was wearing a very tight polo shirt and jodhpurs. She had sparkly false eyelashes on, too.

It was strange seeing James in his best riding clothes – tweed jacket, shirt and tie and jodhpurs – instead of his more familiar torn jeans and scruffy boots. Moth's mane and tail were plaited and we'd all bullied James into trimming the feather off her four white stockings, which were whitened and encased in brushing boots. Her usual striped Indian blanket had been replaced by a neat white nunmah. She'd had a makeover, like my mum.

Bean, too, was done up in her show gear – blue jacket and hat with cream jodhpurs. Katy had her extra-purple cross-country colours on and I, well, I had my usual jodhs and a T-shirt. My outfit was in my backpack.

"Mmmm. That team of chestnuts is a bit scary," I said.

"That lot don't look so hot," James whispered, pointing. A team of assorted hairy ponies sauntered past. They weren't even very clean and the riders all looked half asleep. "If we don't thrash them, I'll eat my hat."

Suddenly, a streak of chestnut and white cantered past. It was Catriona on Bambi. Seeing us, Cat turned and rode over to chat. Well, she chatted to Bean, Katy and James. Her friends. Talk about making a point.

"Who are you, and what have you done with James?" she laughed, referring to James's transformation. Then she turned to me and her face and tone dropped. "I see you're here to make up the numbers."

"You won't say that when we're riding around with our red rosettes," I snapped back. Then I wondered why on earth I'd said such a stupid thing.

"Fat chance!" sneered Cat. "We've got Scott Purnell

on Warrior doing the cross-country and India Hammond on the Dweeb as our show jumping entry – they're both brilliant."

My heart sank. I'd met Scott briefly at school, and he had wanted me to talk to Warrior. But then he'd forgotten, or not bothered, which is hardly surprising as he's a couple of years older than me. Then I realised that it only left Cat to do the Wild Card event. She was in my group. Oh poo!

"Phew, I'm here!" a voice shouted. As Dee pushed her bike across to us, Cat turned Bambi and rode off. Even from the back she looked disdainful. How come she's so good at that?

"Oh good, the groom's arrived," James said gleefully, throwing his reins at her. "Look after Moth, can you Dee? I need to walk the jumping course."

"Oh give us a moment," moaned Dee, "I'm in need of a drink after pedalling all that way. It's all right for you!"

Bluey was the first in our team to do his event, and we watched him quivering with excitement at the start of the cross-country, all keen to get going, Katy a vision in purple.

"Good luck, Katy!" we all shouted. This was the start of our Challenge attempt – how would it go?

Katy grinned at us and I could hear Bluey winding himself up.

"Come on, let me at 'em!" he hissed to himself. And when the starter shouted *GO!* Bluey bounded off in a canter, almost unseating Katy. We watched them leap over the first, bounce over the second, and then they were gone – disappearing with a purple flash into the woods to tackle the rest of the course.

"At least they'll be fine," said Bean. We all agreed with her. Bluey was our trump card, our one sure thing. It was the rest of us who needed help.

Sure enough, Bluey got a splendid clear round with no time faults. Katy's face was one delighted grin – a good impression of a split melon.

"Oh, he was so wonderful," she gushed, sliding out of the saddle and throwing her arms around her pony's sweaty neck. Bluey looked all smug and breathless. "He just ate up all the jumps. He so loves it!"

We all patted Bluey and told them both how great they were. Our Sublime Equine Challenge had got off to a flying start and we all felt totally confident. This was going to be a doddle, I thought. Hickstead here we come! A big fat zero and Bluey's fast time was chalked up on to the scoreboard in the column next to Katy Harris and Blue Haze, Bluey's show name.

We all helped Bean get ready for the dressage and then stood in a supportive huddle as she rode Tiffany round to warm up. I didn't know what Bean was so worried about – she and Tiffany looked every inch a dressage pair, if you didn't count Tiff muttering about something spooky over there and a balloon behind her and what was that woman with the dog doing. Bean rides so well, and I could see them impressing the judges no end, much more than Drum and me, anyway. Once she was in the arena, I was sure she'd be OK.

Leanne and Mr Higgins had just done their test and as they rode out and the next rider rode in, Leanne steered her dun gelding over to Bean and we could see them talking, with Leanne pointing at Tiffany. As Leanne rode off we could tell something was wrong – very wrong; Bean was close to tears. Stopping in front of us, she threw the reins on to her pony's golden neck, her shoulders slumped in defeat.

"We can't do this!" she said.

"Of course you can," said Katy, soothingly.

"You'll be fine," I said. "You were really great in practice."

"No, you don't get it, WE CAN'T DO THIS!" Bean repeated, through clenched teeth.

"Why?" we all said.

"What did Leanne say?" asked James.

"Leanne knows the rules. She's just told me that all dressage entrants have to wear the right tack as stated under British Dressage rules, or they'll be disqualified – and that means the team will be disqualified, too."

"So what do you need?" I asked, running my eyes over Tiffany. "Is your bit wrong? It's just an eggbutt snaffle. You haven't got a martingale, which isn't allowed . . . what's the problem?"

"It's the noseband," said Bean, her bottom lip trembling. "Tiffany has to wear a noseband – and you know what happens when she does. The whole team's going to be out of the competition!"

Chapter Five

I stared at Tiffany's naked nose. Tiffany hadn't worn a noseband since I'd overheard her telling Bambi about her noseband phobia, something to do with an injury in her youth. Ever since the day I'd told Bean it was the noseband that made Tiffany shake her head uncontrollably, the offending piece of tack had been dumped. We were all so used to seeing Tiffany's naked face, we hadn't given it a second thought.

Until now.

"Why didn't Leanne say something at the yard?" asked James.

"She thought I was still doing the show jumping!" replied Bean. "We never do dressage! Not since the last time when I lost my way – that was way before you told me about Tiffany's noseband phobia, Pia."

"I'll get you Bluey's cavesson," Katy said, already

running toward the ponies.

"Fat lot of good that will do!" grumbled Bean. "Tiff will just shake her head all the way round her test. At least it won't matter if I forget the moves!"

Sliding off her pony, she burst into tears. Horrified, I looked at James who put his arm around her and said quietly, "Oh come on Bean, it'll be OK . . ."

"Don't, James!" Bean sniffed, pulling away. "I never wanted to do the dressage – no-one cared how I felt, and now it's my fault we'll be disqualified."

Bean was right, we had pushed her into it and ignored her protests – we'd been so sure she'd been exaggerating and had focused only on how well she usually rode. How well she rode was immaterial if she couldn't remember the test, or Tiffany's headshaking returned.

Pushing James out of the way I put my arm on Bean's shoulder, hoping she wouldn't turn on me. She didn't. "Bean, don't cry, please. I'll talk to Tiffany; she'll try her best for a few minutes, I'm sure."

Bean wiped her nose on her black jacket, leaving a nasty, snotty trail.

I got close to Tiffany and whispered in her ear. "Tiffany, don't freak but you need to wear a noseband for the dressage test – it's just for a few minutes. Please,

please, don't headshake! Poor Bean's really upset and it would mean a lot to her."

Tiffany turned and looked at me, the fear obvious in her eyes. "Please don't make me wear one. Please! I get flashbacks to when I had one on too tightly, before I was with Bean. It hurt so much. It just freaks me out."

"I know, but we really need you to do this. You can do it, I know you can. We'll put it on loosely – it's just a cavesson. Please try." A cavesson noseband doesn't actually do anything, it just hangs there. I didn't know why dressage rules state that horses and ponies have to wear something which does nothing, but hey-ho, it was a bit late to be challenging it now.

"What's she saying?" sniffed Bean, wrapping a supportive arm around her pony's neck.

I told her.

"Please Tiffany – I don't want to do this either, but it's for the team!" Bean whispered to her.

A breathless Katy arrived with Bluey's cavesson noseband and we threaded it on to Tiffany's bridle. The palomino stiffened and held her breath as we did it up as loosely as we could.

"Promise me you'll get this off as soon as I come out!" Tiffany said.

"Of course, the very second you're finished," I promised.

"Poor Tiffany, I'm so, so sorry," sniffed Bean, mounting and heading for the arena just as the announcer called Charlotte Beanie and Tiffany's Golden Trinket to the dressage arena.

We all held our breath.

The best bits about Bean and Tiffany's test were the start and finish. The bits in between were worse than we could have imagined. Tiffany broke pace at canter and, unable to help herself, she shook her head violently several times. Bean, upset and trembling, forgot the test three times – just as she promised she would – and missed a whole chunk out altogether.

"Well done!" we all chimed loyally, trying to be supportive as they came out. I rushed to strip the noseband off Tiffany's bridle.

"Oh, that was hateful," shuddered Tiffany. She had obviously been very brave about it, considering.

"That test was crap," hissed James.

"We know, but shut up about it!" I hissed back.

Dressage is scored as a percentage – anything over sixty percent is considered quite good. Each movement is marked out of ten, with the overall percentage score worked out later. Bean obviously lost quite a number of points for not completing several of the required movements.

"Thirty-two percent!" wailed Bean when she read her score on the board. "It must have looked even worse than it felt."

"Don't worry, yours can be the score we drop," said James, tactlessly.

"I think you did brilliantly, under the circumstances," Katy said firmly, and we all agreed. Secretly, I could see our chances of getting a qualifying place towards the Hickstead final this time were racing downhill. Fast.

I couldn't help noticing that Leanne had scored seventy-nine percent, a fantastic score and in the lead so far. We went back to the ponies to nurse our hurts. Bean's dressage score was a blow, but we couldn't do anything about it. It wasn't like she hadn't warned us. We had insisted she'd be all right. We'd been wrong. OK, we could drop her score, but it put a lot of pressure on the rest of the team to do well.

"You and Moth had better leave all the jumps up since you nicked that event from Bean," I warned James.

"Thank goodness you're all back!" said Dee, tangled up in reins. "Perhaps now I can go to the loo. Can you

NOT leave me three ponies all at once? How did Tiffany and Bean do? Was the noseband all right?"

"No!" said Bean, and told Dee all about it. It was strange hearing someone moaning to Dee for a change.

When it was James's turn to jump, Bean and I followed him over to the arena, leaving Katy and Dee with the ponies. India Hammond from *Team SLIC* was flying around the course on the Dweeb, her careful, flea-bitten grey pony. Blonde and very pretty, India looked every inch the part in her navy jacket and pink tie.

"She's really good," hissed Bean. "She's been show jumping since she was tiny."

I could hear the Dweeb talking himself round: *Hang on India, this is a tricky one, now this oxer, yes! Where to now? Oh, I see, the wall, here we go, toes tucked up . . .*

I noticed James gazing at India. Well, she was a bit of a stunner. I couldn't help feeling a pang of jealousy and I wished I looked like India, all blonde and petite, instead of having a mane of unruly reddish brown hair which matched Drummer's coat. When India rode past us after her faultless clear round, she smiled at James and waved. We watched her ride back to her team mates, who all clapped her on the back and cheered.

For the Sublime Equine Challenge, there was to be

no jump-off – everyone had one chance to aim for a fast clear round. Every fence down added ten seconds to the round, so accuracy was vital. James and Moth did not copy India's example. Although fast, Moth clipped a pole on the oxer, and then she managed to dislodge a brick in the wall, adding twenty seconds to her time and putting her way down the line. We weren't exactly shining.

"Never mind," I said to James, who was all apologetic. "You did your best."

"I think I'm still making poor Moth drop her hind legs," James said, hanging his head.

It was my turn. Could I make up some lost ground for the team?

"Go out and knock the judges dead!" whispered James, as I got Drummer dressed up in his red and yellow outfit. Epona was firmly zipped into the pocket of my jodhpurs. Our whole routine depended on her being with us.

"I'll never forgive you for this," hissed Drummer.

"Oh don't be so melodramatic!" I told him, tying the ear protectors to his headcollar. "Four minutes, that's all!"

I gave James the CD of medieval-sounding lute and piano music for my routine and he went over to give it to the steward. Luckily, with so many events going on, there was hardly anyone around the wild card ring, which was a huge relief. I dragged Drummer over and as we got there, I could see Cat performing her routine with Bambi.

Cat was long-reining her skewbald mare. She'd threaded two long lines through the stirrups on Bambi's saddle, and was steering Bambi around in circles and figures-of-eights. Then she got Bambi going sideways, and then backwards. To finish, Bambi stood up straight in front of the judges and Cat came up beside her and saluted. It looked very neat and impressive, with Cat in her riding clothes and Bambi with her white patches gleaming, her chestnut patches shining in the sun, her mane and tail fiercely plaited.

My heart sank. Why hadn't I thought of something as classy as that? Why had I thought up something that made me and Drummer look like fools? Our routine suddenly seemed childish and I wished with all my heart that we didn't have to go in and perform it. Drum had been right all along. It was a stupid, stupid routine. What had I been thinking of in my amateurish home-made dress and wimple? This Challenge thing was turning into a nightmare. Why had we ever thought it was a good idea? However had we expected to do well? What had we been thinking off?

"It's your turn, break a leg!" hissed James, giving me a push. We had to pass Cat and Bambi as we jingle-jangled our way to the middle of the ring and I heard Cat snort with laughter when she caught sight of us.

Oh, *double poo.*

"Come on then," sighed Drum, "let's get it over with."

I nodded to the judges and one of them started the CD.

"OK, Drum, let's give it our all!" I whispered to him as the music blared out. Boy, it was loud. We'd never had it on that loud at home when we'd been practising.

"OK, circle around me," I said to Drum.

"What?" Drummer said, planted to the spot.

"Circle around me!" I said louder.

"You'll have to speak up," shouted Drummer, shaking his head and ringing all the bells.

"Just do what we did at home!" I yelled.

"I can't hear you!" Drummer replied.

It was hopeless! The combination of the music and Drum's ear protectors with bells on made it impossible for him to hear my directions. Somehow, we muddled through, but it wasn't anything like as polished as it had been in practice at home in the paddock. We went wrong, we turned away when we should have turned towards each other, and we finished at different times before the music stopped, bowing out of sync. I couldn't wait to get out of the arena.

"Thank you!" shouted one of the judges in a bored voice, obviously relieved that our performance was over.

We came third from last.

"Drum couldn't hear me," I explained.

"Maybe you should take those ear things off," suggested Dee.

"Good idea!" snorted Drummer.

"Oh, you heard that all right!" I said crossly.

"Well, now there's no music thundering out like we're at Glastonbury!" he replied. "Maybe you should think of adapting our routine with all these bells ringing, how about we change it to the Hunchback of Notre Dame? You could stuff a cushion up the back of your dress."

"It just needs adapting, that's all," Katy told me, unaware of Drummer's comments. "And we ALL need to practise a bit more. I mean, we didn't think we were going to win, did we?"

I remembered my boast to Cat about red rosettes.

Then I saw her on Bambi. A yellow rosette fluttered from Bambi's bridle.

"Oh look," said Bean, "Leanne and Cat's team has come third."

She rode Tiffany over and was soon congratulating Cat, who was beaming. I could hear Tiffany and Bambi talking – they're quite good chums and often graze in the field together.

"You did well!" said Tiffany.

"Yes, we've got a strong team. How's your team panning out?"

"Mmmm, well, you know what it's like, the humans are all keen so you have to put up a bit of a show, don't you? I don't really do dressage, as you know, AND it turns out I have to wear a noseband, which is the final straw and – ooh, WHAT'S THAT? Oh, it's OK, it's just a burger carton – so I'm hoping – well, Drum, Moth and I all are – that we don't go through to the finals, especially as we don't get much in the way of thanks from anyone. It's all about them, them, them. We'd love to nip the whole thing – LOOK OUT . . . oh no, it's all right, it's just a small child with an ice cream – in the bud right here. Of course, we can't get Bluey on board, he won't make a hash-up of the cross-country whatever you say to him. Oh, by the way, Drummer keeps asking me to put in a good word for him."

"Oh don't remind me. He's a right pain. As if I'm going to fall for a bay who wears bells on his ears!"

"You are hard on him – he's OK really. But who's that gorgeous black creature on your team, the one who's doing the cross-country?"

"You mean Warrior? Mmmm, he is yummy, isn't he? I wouldn't mind if he fancied me. I don't think I'm his type – he might go for you, though. All blonde and skinny."

Shutting my ears to their conversation, I took all Drummer's jester-ware off. He shook himself and sneezed.

"Can we go home now?"

"I know what you're doing – you and Moth and Tiffany," I said menacingly.

"Don't know what you're talking about!"

We rode home in gloomy silence. Only Bluey was happy – as he always is when he's jumped a cross-country round. I could hear him talking the other ponies through it, jump-by-jump. The other ponies were bored into silence.

"You know that Leanne and Cat are half-way to qualifying, don't you?" said Bean.

"Yes, thank you, we know," I said.

"That chavvy team, the one with the hairy ponies and the dozy riders, they came second. SECOND!" wailed James.

"Serves us right for underestimating them," said Katy. "What do you want with your hat, James? Fries? Salad?"

"Oh, you're funny!" said James.

"It's not even worth bothering to go to another qualifier," mumbled Bean.

"Of course it is!" said Katy.

"You would say that, you did really well. The rest of us are pants," I reminded her.

"You've got a good routine," said James, "it just needs a few tweaks."

"No-one liked it. Everyone sniggered," I moaned.

"I'll work the CD player next time. And if you make some adjustments to Drum's ear covers so he can hear you, that will sort it!"

"Yes, Pia," added Bean, "you're the only one who can do it – although I don't see how Tiff and I can do another dressage test in a noseband. It's impossible!"

"It's not only the noseband that's the trouble," said James, "you lost your way twice."

I cringed. Talk about tactless.

"I can't remember dressage tests – I told you all that," Bean said with exaggerated calm, keeping her cool.

"I can remember them," I said, desperately, wondering if it wasn't too late to swap events with Bean. It was as if Katy could read my mind.

"We can't change events half-way through. The rules say the same team members have to do the same events throughout the competition. We just have to try harder next time," she said. As Katy was the only member of our team who'd been any good and, it appeared, had bothered to read the rules, we couldn't really argue.

"It's a shame you didn't know the rule about the noseband," James muttered.

"We weren't exactly Team Tremendous, were we?" grumbled Bean.

"Team Useless, more like," agreed James. "Perhaps we should call ourselves Team Desperate, or Team Argument, or Team Only-Here-To-Make-Up-The-Numbers!"

"Oh that's the spirit!" said Katy, sarcastically.

"It doesn't matter how hard we try if the ponies aren't on board," I said, and relayed Tiffany and Bambi's conversation.

"Oh!" said Katy, lost for words for once.

"Well," I said grimly, "we only have one more chance

68

to stay in the competition. If we don't come in the first three in the next qualifier, the decision will be taken away from us. We'll be out, whether we like it or not!"

Chapter Six

That evening, I met Mum's new boyfriend, Brian. With the day having gone so badly, I wasn't in the mood to show myself off as the model daughter.

"This is Pia," said Mum. "Pia, I'd like you to meet Brian."

"Good evening, Pia."

"Umm, hello," I mumbled. Brian was quite tall. He had sandy-coloured hair, the sort of hair that looks like cotton wool, you know what I mean? Sort of undefined strands, just stuck on his head in a blob like doll hair. His beard was grey and short and trimmed. His left ear lobe sported a silver stud which he was like miles too old for. What was that about?

"Pia's been looking forward to meeting you," Mum lied. I smiled. Well it seemed expected.

"I understand you have a pony," said Brian. "I used

to ride when I was younger, but I gave it up when I discovered girls." He looked across at Mum and grinned at her. She giggled back, blushing. I didn't really think I could handle all this after the day I'd had. I thought furiously for something to say. What do grown-ups say when they meet?

"What do you do for a living, Brian?"

"I'm a teacher. English. Do you enjoy English at school, Pia?"

OK, you can think I'm negative if you want (some of Drummer's attitude rubs off), but don't you think that teachers never give it a rest? I mean, they just have to be right all the time, don't they? I prayed that Brian wasn't a typical teacher, because that would be soooo irritating.

But it wasn't long before he started.

"Brian and I went to a fabulous pub by the river – I must take you there, Pia, you'd love it. Such a pretty place," Mum told me.

"Can you remember the name of the river, Sue?" Brian asked with a smarmy smile. "I did tell you."

See what I mean? *"My mum's a grown-up!"* I wanted to scream. *"She wasn't on a field trip – it was a date, for goodness' sake!"*

"Oh, no, I can't. Sorry!" giggled Mum.

"It's detention for you, young lady!" joked Brian.

Pass the sick bag, I thought. Luckily, they left soon after for dinner at some restaurant Mum has always liked the look of. As soon as they'd gone, I rang Bean.

"Look," I said, as soon as she answered, "we have to have a pow-wow tomorrow at the yard and discuss where the team goes from here. I think I need to have a word with the ponies. See you there at nine?"

"OK, sounds like a plan," Bean said. "What are you doing now? There's a great film on in ten minutes, Channel Four."

"My mum's just gone on a date," I told her. "You wouldn't believe the geek she's seeing now. Can you ring Katy and tell her about tomorrow? I'll call James."

James wasn't answering his mobile, so I left a text message. Then I cooked myself a jacket potato with cheese and beans, watched the film Bean had recommended, which made me laugh despite our disastrous day, and took myself off to bed before Brian brought Mum home. I couldn't face another dose of him.

The next morning, Mum insisted on asking my opinion of Brian. I so hate the post-mortem of the first meeting. Remembering I had promised to support her in her dating, I put on my ever-so-sincere-if-you-don't-look-too-close face which I've had rather a lot of practice at recently.

"What's important, Mum, is that you like him."

"I do, he's very attentive."

I didn't want to think about Brian being attentive to my mum. I cycled to the yard with Epona in my pocket, trying to put all unwanted images out of my mind. Katy and Bean were already there so we pulled all the ponies in from the field, including Moth.

"Are you going to read them the riot act?" asked Bean.

"That's the plan!" I told her, grimly. Towing the ponies in behind us, we found James had arrived.

"Come on," I said, "let's take this lot somewhere where we won't be disturbed."

"What are we going to do?" he joked. "Give them a damn good thrashing?"

"Don't say that!" cried Katy, hugging Bluey protectively. As if we would!

"Oh come on, Katy, it was a joke," said James. "I don't even carry a whip on Moth, you know that!"

"It wasn't funny!" said Katy, furious with James.

We took them all behind Bambi, Drummer and Moth's stables. Unfortunately, there was rather a lot of grass growing there.

"Oooh, this is the sort of ticking-off I like!" cried Drum, dropping his head to graze. Tiffany and Bluey followed his lead; only Moth stood all polite as usual, waiting for James to tell her it was OK to do the same.

I hauled Drummer's head up. "Now look you lot," I began, "we know you're not making any effort with this Sublime Equine Challenge."

"That's not fair!" wailed Bluey.

"Oh, sorry Bluey," I said, "I know you are. You're the exception. Your mates here are deliberately sabotaging any effort to qualify in an attempt to cut down on work."

"Are you?" asked Bluey, in wide-eyed amazement. He is such an honest pony.

"Oh, come on," said Drummer, defensively. "I was dressed up to look like the village idiot. No wonder I'm not keen."

"I wore the noseband under duress, and I take exception to your accusations," Tiffany said, huffily. "Is that a . . . oh no, it's just an old bucket!" she added, her indignation in ruins.

"Yes, you did," I agreed. "But I heard you talking to Bambi, you can't deny it!"

"What's she saying?" said Bean.

Moth said nothing. As usual. I couldn't give Epona

to James with Bean and Katy there. He would have to get her feedback later.

"How could you not try?" asked Bluey, looking crestfallen. "I jumped my heart out for the team."

Tiffany shifted her hooves and Drummer looked into the distance. Then Tiffany grunted and spoke.

"Actually," she said, huffily, "Drum and I think we're being taken for granted."

"What do you mean?" I said, baffled.

"What are they saying?" Bean asked again.

"That's right," interrupted Drummer. "You want us to do these things, but do we hear any word of thanks? Any praise? No! It's just moan, moan, moan. Katy's always appreciative of Bluey's hard work and you can see the results for yourselves."

I was stunned.

"What's the news?" James said, hopping from one foot to the other. "Come *on* Pia, tell us!"

"Er . . ." I didn't know where to start. A very uncomfortable feeling grew in my stomach. It got worse and worse. Drum was right, I hadn't given him any encouragement at all – I had just grumbled and moaned all the time. I felt really ashamed. I took a deep breath.

"It's our fault," I told the others.

"Ours? How?" Bean asked.

"Why?" said James.

"They say they never get any thanks for their efforts, that we don't appreciate them. We just moan."

There was a stunned silence.

"Oh, Bluey, I'm sorry!" said Katy, throwing her arms around his neck and smothering him with kisses.

"Actually, Katy, the ponies say you're the only one who's OK. And you are."

"You are really nice to Bluey," added Bean, thoughtfully. "And positive."

"Looks like it's up to us to change things, then," said James.

"I'm so sorry Tiff," said Bean, stroking Tiffany's golden neck. "I promise I'll be more like Katy."

"That will be nice," sniffed Tiffany. "I'll try harder, too – even with the noseband if I have to."

"She's going all out next time," I assured Bean.

"Oh, good girl, have all the grass you want!" cried Bean, patting Tiffany's neck like mad. I turned to Drummer.

"I'm really sorry, Drum. You're right, and I've been totally in the wrong. Can we start again? We've got a week to sort things out before the next qualifier."

Drummer looked at Bluey and Tiffany, and then me.

He gave a huge sigh. "Oh, OK, I'll be magnificent next time," he said. "I'll perform like Trigger, or Champion the Wonder Horse. I'll be so brilliant, I'll be nominated for an Oscar. Now can I get my head down before that greedy Tiffany eats all this grass?"

"Fill your boots!" I told him.

When the grass looked like a flock of sheep had spent the night there, we took the ponies back to their stables and I handed Epona to James when no-one was looking.

"Your turn to have a word, find out Moth's take on it all," I told him. Five minutes later and James was back.

"We're good," he said. "Moth's jumping faults were genuine but I could be a bit more thankful, too, apparently. She said we have to remember we're a team."

I felt so utterly guilty. How awful to be reminded by our own ponies about how we were supposed to get the most out of them. In our excitement and nervousness about the Sublime Equine Challenge, we'd overlooked the fact that ponies, just like people, respond to praise and encouragement, not negativity. We so totally had to remember that and stop moaning all the time.

Drummer and I practised our routine again, and I

made sure I was much more polite and asked his opinion on certain movements. He even had some good suggestions. Tiffany and Bean did some schooling (minus the noseband!) with Katy and James offering useful advice from the fence, and they all made a real fuss of Tiff. Both ponies were co-operation personified. It was so great! In the afternoon, we all went for a hairy ride in the woods to let off some steam. The ponies loved it, and so did we!

"OK," said James, pulling an over-excited Moth up after we'd raced each other to the lake, "we're good to go all-out at the next qualifier. Let's go for it!"

We all gave a high-five and whooped with delight. Bring it on! We were sure to do better the next time round. The ponies' pep talk had definitely sorted us all out!

We rode back to the yard with Tiffany, now thoroughly excited, going sideways and setting Drum off. It took ages to settle them down and as we walked through the woods, Katy brought up the subject of our team name, insisting it would help the team spirit.

"I don't get Cat and Leanne's team name," said Bean. "I mean SLIC, what does that mean?"

"It's their names — Scott, Leanne, India and Catriona," Katy explained.

I thought that was clever – and lucky that it worked.

"Well we could do that. How about we're Team BPKJ?" suggested Bean.

"That's gibberish!" snorted Katy.

"That's it, Team Gibberish!" yelled James.

"I think we need to come up with something snappy. Something that sums up what we're about," Katy said.

"So we're back to Team Useless," said James. Katy glared at him.

"Or we could be ironic," James said. "How about the Fantastic Four?"

"That's not ironic," said Bean, "that's just lying."

"But maybe if we give ourselves something to live up to, it might not turn out ironic at all," suggested Katy.

"As long as we don't have T-shirts," I said. "I don't want to walk around with that on my back."

"Can anyone think of anything better?" asked James. No-one said a word.

"That's it then, the Fantastic Four it is!" said Katy, as we rode into the yard.

"Excuse me," said a voice. It was Drummer and he wasn't very happy. "There are eight of us in this team. I can see our little pep talk has had very little effect."

"What's your point?" I said, confused. I could see

Katy and Bean looking at me. James had ridden off to Moth's stable and was out of earshot.

"Yes," added Tiffany, "what about us?"

"You're doing it again," said Bluey, shaking his head.

"What's wrong now?" Katy asked.

"We're can't be the Fantastic Four," I told her. "There are eight of us."

Bean's hand flew to her mouth. "Oh no, we're in trouble again!" she cried.

"Oh, sorry Bluey. You're right!" exclaimed Katy.

"Can we be the Fantastic Eight, then?" I asked. It didn't sound as catchy.

"Hardly," said Drummer, in disgust.

"We can be the Great Eight," suggested Bluey.

"Brilliant!" I said, and told the others. They agreed and Bean trotted Tiffany over to tell James there'd been a change of plan. Already!

As I took my feet out of my stirrups, my mobile went off. Sliding to the ground, I saw it was Dad calling. We hadn't spoken for a while.

"Hi, Dad!" I said.

"Hello, Pumpkin – how's my best girl?" he boomed. I had to hold the phone at arm's length, he was so loud.

"OK, thanks. How are you. And Lyn?" I remembered to add.

"Yes, we're fine thanks, love. We'd like to come over and see you – and hey, you'll love this . . ."

I held my breath.

". . . Lyn's taking up horse riding."

There was a pause for dramatic effect. I said nothing – due to the fact that I was totally stunned, my mouth wide open like a landed fish.

"I said she might as well try it out on old Drummer before she gets all the gear in case she doesn't like it," Dad continued. "If we come over tomorrow, then Lyn can have a ride on Drummer. What do you say?"

Skinny Lynny, on Drummer? What a cheek! But then, I could hardly say no, could I? I got my gaping mouth sorted and went to say, OK then, but it came out as a sort of mouse squeak.

"Right then, it's a date!" said Dad. He never seems to understand that I might have plans. It's as though I'd been moping around, with nothing to do, just waiting for him to phone so I can let his horrid, skinny girlfriend ride MY pony. Then I remembered that I'd promised myself to make an effort with Skinny Lynny, and what had I just learnt from the ponies?

"Er . . ." I said.

"We'll meet you at Drummer's at eleven o'clock

tomorrow. I'm looking forward to seeing you, Pumpkin, we both are!"

He rang off.

"Did I hear right?" enquired a wide-eyed Drummer, his head up like an indignant llama. "Do I take it I'm giving pony rides tomorrow?"

"Yes," I told him. "And before you get all huffy about it, remember that my dad pays for your keep so play ball or you could find yourself in one of the small ads in the local paper."

"No need for threats," Drummer sniffed. "I knew your positivity wouldn't last."

Oh poo, I thought. It seemed no sooner had we sorted out one problem, another galloped up to fill its space.

Chapter Seven

It was almost a quarter to twelve when they arrived. I'd had Drummer tacked up for over half-an-hour. You can imagine how he felt about that!

"Hi there, Pumpkin!" shouted Dad, once he'd parked the car next to Sophie's luxury horsebox. I'm probably getting a bit old to be called that. I mean, it had been OK when I was six. Would Dad still be calling me Pumpkin when I was sixteen, or eighteen, or really old, say twenty-one?

When Skinny Lynny got out of the car I couldn't stop my mouth from becoming a black hole. She was wearing bronze-coloured breeches and the latest Sublime Equine lime green polo-neck shirt. Long, leather riding boots made her walk as though she had no knees and her long, blonde hair spilled out from under a top-of-the-range blue velvet riding hat. I thought this session on Drum was a try-out to decide whether she was going to take up riding? She looked fairly committed to me. At least six-hundred pounds committed, and my dad would have paid for it. I heard a gulp behind me.

"Clock that!" Drummer exclaimed. "I thought you said she couldn't ride?"

"She can't!" I hissed back.

"Doesn't our Lyn look the part then, eh?" said Dad, looking all pleased and proud with his trophy girlfriend in her over-the-top get-up.

"I thought you'd be a bit smarter, Pia," scolded Lyn, looking me up and down. What a cheek! I was dressed in jodhpurs and polo-shirt.

"I think I might enjoy this," chuckled Drummer.

"Drummer . . ." I growled, in a warning voice. Skinny Lynny tipped her head to one side and smiled.

"Dear Pia," she said in the sort of voice you use to tell tiny children that their teddies will cry if they don't eat up all their greens, "are the ponies talking to you again?"

Skinny Lynny had never really believed that I could hear what horses and ponies were saying. She'd always treated me as thought I was making it up, or even a bit bonkers. I didn't really care whether she believed me or not. Impressing Skinny Lynny wasn't a priority of mine.

"Now," said Dad, rubbing his hands together, "I can't wait to see the future showjumper of the year on board."

I led Drummer to the outdoor school and over to the mounting block, showing Skinny Lynny how to mount. After a few squeaks and squeals, and a shove from me, she was soon sitting in Drum's saddle, looking scared stiff.

"It's very high up," she said.

"No, it isn't," I mumbled, sulkily.

"You look fantastic in the saddle, darling," shouted Dad from the other side of the fence.

"No, she doesn't," I argued. Skinny Lynny sat stiffly with her bottom jutting out and her heels clamped into Drummer's sides.

"Now sit up and tuck your tail under you," I told her.

"I haven't got a tail," said Skinny Lynny, breathless at the suggestion.

"I know, but make like you do. That's better. Now breathe."

"Oh, I was holding my breath!" gasped Skinny Lynny. "How did you know that?"

"All beginners do it. OK, don't rest your hands on the saddle, carry them like this . . . Good. Now put all your weight down your legs and into your heels. Let them drop. Relax . . ." I wobbled her legs until they softened. "Now I'm going to lead Drum around and I want you to stay in that position."

Drum took a step forward. Skinny Lynny squealed. I just spotted the wicked gleam in his eye as Drum shook his head, which had Skinny Lynny clutching his mane, squeaking like a guinea-pig.

This wasn't going well.

"Don't squeal, you'll scare Drummer," I said. Skinny Lynny looked at me wide-eyed and terrified. "It's OK, he's not easily scared," I reassured her. "But you need to be quiet."

"Will he throw me off?" she whispered.

I so wanted to say yes. Instead, I said, "No, no, he's a pussycat, honestly!" as Drummer – encouraged by the success of his head shaking – put in a hop and squealed himself.

Skinny Lynny squeaked and yelled, "Make him stop or I'll get off!"

"Oh, this is going to be such fun," sniggered Drummer. Secretly, I agreed with him. Skinny was hopeless. I mean, we'd only taken three fairy steps and she was all for throwing in the towel.

"Just sit up and Drummer will be fine," I told her. "Honestly, I won't let go of him."

Dad climbed through the fence and came over.

"Are you all right, darling?" he said, all concerned. He wasn't talking to me.

"This horse is dangerous," Skinny replied accusingly, "and Pia can't control him."

"Of course he isn't and of course I can," I said.

"I could be!" threatened Drummer, menacingly.

"Come on Lyn, you've got all the gear now. You might at least walk round," Dad encouraged.

"Well, I'll try to be brave," Skinny Lynny replied, smiling at Dad.

"That's my girl!" beamed Dad.

I thought I was going to throw up. I mean, it was hardly heroic, plodding around with me hanging on to Drummer's reins.

So we walked around, and the squeaking died down – at least it did from the saddle. Drum had realised he was on to a good thing, however, and as soon as I took my eye off him, he put in a hop, or he threw his head down to scratch his knee, or he shook his head and squealed. Every time, Skinny Lynny clutched his mane and caught her breath or she squealed back. It was like the clash of the squeaky toys.

"Shall we try a trot?" I said, wearily.

"Is that fast?" Skinny gasped.

"Fast-*er*," I said.

"Oh, OK, second gear. All right," she agreed.

I explained what trotting would feel like and got her to hold the front of the saddle.

"Keep your heels down and sit up tall," I said. "Here we go – nice and gently!" I growled at Drummer.

"Tee-hee!" chuckled Drum, and he bounded forward into a trot. Skinny yelled for him to stop, stop, STOP! And Drum obliged, very suddenly, snorting when Skinny landed on his neck.

"Trotting's awful!" she gulped. "How can this be so difficult – it looks so easy!"

"Yeah, well, everyone thinks that but it takes a long time to learn," I said. "Shall we have another go, now you know what to expect?"

We did. We even managed half a circuit in trot. After that, I decided to stick to walking and got Skinny Lynny to steer instead. That went rather well, and Skinny Lynny managed a smile. Once she'd learned how to stop, she was much more confident.

"Come on, now," Dad called, already bored. "We don't want to be late for lunch, Lyn." I remembered that he'd never been very keen on watching me ride, either.

"Oh, hold on," said Drummer, and he lifted his tail and dropped a large poo on the sand.

"Oh that's so awful!" moaned drama queen Skinny, dropping one rein and wafting her hand in front of her face.

"It's only pony poo," I muttered.

I got Skinny Lynny to lead Drummer back to the yard. Of course, he grabbed hold of the bit and dragged her over to the feed room, and I had to rescue her. Then he rubbed his head on her, leaving brown hairs all over the lime Sublime Equine polo top and concluded by scoring a direct hit on her foot with his near front hoof, offering Skinny Lynny yet another screaming opportunity.

"Oooops!" exclaimed Drummer, all innocent.

"I don't know that Drummer is a very safe pony for you, Pia," mused Dad, massaging Skinny Lynny's foot. "He seems a bit wild. I can get you a quieter pony, if you like."

"Of course Drummer isn't wild," I told him. "Honestly Dad, he's just playing up because he knows Lyn isn't very experienced. All ponies do it."

"Well, if you change your mind . . ." Dad continued.

"Stop it!" I hissed, looking Drummer in the eye. "I know what you're doing, but it'll backfire on you. She's not an X-Box game."

"I don't know how you put up with the awful horsey smell around here," moaned Skinny Lynny, screwing up her nose.

"Horses smell OK!" I said.

"But all that manure – from the muck heap. I mean, it's steaming," said Skinny. "It can't be healthy."

"It's fine. No-one notices it after a while," I said, firmly. Now she was going to get Drum sold on the grounds of health and safety. Honestly!

"If you think that's bad . . ." began Drummer, lifting his tail and letting out a long, and very smelly, fart.

Skinny put her hand over her nose and whimpered. I couldn't understand it, I mean, she lives with my dad and he's much worse than Drum when he's had a curry.

"Well, goodbye Drummer, thank you for the ride," Skinny Lynny said, patting Drummer on the forehead. Drum blinked dramatically every time her hand connected. Pat-blink, pat-blink, pat-blink.

"Bye-bye, Lynne!" Skinny Lynny said in a pretend Drummer voice. "I did enjoy you riding me!"

"Oh pur-leeese!" said Drummer, rolling his eyes and backing into his box to escape.

Skinny wiped her hands on a nearby bale of hay, anxious to get any Drummer-scent and Drummer-dirt off them. I don't know why, Drum smells great – when he's not farting.

We went off for lunch in the pub. And, get this, Skinny Lynny didn't even get hat-hair! Peeling off her riding hat, she just shook her head and looked gorgeous. How does that work? When I take my riding hat off, my hair's stuck to my head like it's been glued there.

All the men in the pub swivelled around to stare at Skinny in her breeches and boots. I could see Dad puffing out his chest in pride, like he was personally responsible for Skinny's figure. I suppose that's why he ran off with her in the first place. The thought of my dad behaving like those lecherous men in the pub made me feel a bit strange. I mean, yuk!

"So what's on your agenda this summer holidays, Pia," asked Dad. I told them about the Sublime Equine Challenge, and how Drum and I were the Wild Card. I sort of glossed over how badly our team had performed in the first qualifier, concentrating instead on our plans to get to the Hickstead final.

After lunch, Dad dropped me back at the yard. "We'll have to do this again," he said.

"Mmmm," agreed Skinny. "Now I've got all the gear, I shall need to use it!"

I waved and sighed with relief as I watched the car bounce down the drive and away. Then I remembered how I had promised myself I'd make more of an effort with Skinny Lynny.

And how I had failed.

Again.

Chapter Eight

Having had our confidence shaken so much at the first qualifier, we were all very nervous at the second, held at Beeches Riding School, even though the ponies had promised to do their best. But we were all determined to big them up, whatever the outcome. If we didn't make the first three this time, it was the end of the road as far as our Hickstead ambitions went.

Beeches was miles away, so by the time we'd hacked there we were all pretty well warmed-up. I had our outfits in my backpack, so they were a bit creased, but we had to go with it. I wished I'd asked Dee to bring them with her – her mum was dropping her off by car after her schooling session with Dolly. Her HOYS campaign was in full swing and she'd just missed qualifying at her last show by one place. Not for anything would I have swapped places with Dee in the horsebox on that return journey with her miffed mum. Can you imagine?

My mum couldn't come because she was on a date with Brian.

This time, Drum and I were first to go, in the Wild Card event. As I waited in the collecting ring, smoothing down the creases in my skirt and trying not to look at the other teams. I whispered to Drummer, reminding him of his promise.

"Stop worrying," he said. "I'll be an absolute pro. Honest. Your wimple's wonky, by the way – you're letting me down."

I pulled the conical hat straight. There was a stiff breeze, and the chiffon scarf kept blowing across my face. My yellow dress threatened to trip me up. I saw Katy, Bean and Dee-Dee with Bluey, Tiffany and Moth, all grinning and giving me the thumbs up sign from the ropes. Well, the humans were, the ponies obviously couldn't because they don't have thumbs.

"The next competitors are Pia Edwards and Drummer, for the Great Eight," the announcer managed to say without sniggering, which was impressive. Drum and I walked into the ring and faced the judges – three of them standing with clipboards, looking all stern and important. I nodded towards James and he started the CD player. It was now or never!

Drummer was as good as his word. He twirled, he shuffled, he did exactly what we'd practised and what I asked him to do. He even shook his head a couple of times to get the bells going. At the end, we bowed to the judges and I could see them all smiling broadly – they even clapped.

"You STAR!" I hissed to Drummer, patting him like mad as we left the ring.

"Told you," he said, smugly.

"Oh, well done, you were both brilliant!" squealed Katy, peeling off Drum's leg bandages.

"Good old Drummer!" cried Dee-Dee, forcing pony cubes into my pony's willing mouth.

"Not so much of the old," Drummer mumbled, shaking his head as I peeled off his ear protectors.

"Good job, Pia!" said James.

"Now you all have to be fabulous, too!" I laughed, relieved our part was over. It was a tremendous start. Our score was fourteen out of twenty – not bad!

I caught sight of Cat and Bambi performing their polished routine, their team mates cheering at the end. But we couldn't stay long, because it was Bean's turn to perform her dressage.

"I'm so nervous, look!" she said, thrusting wobbly

hands out in front of her. "What if we mess up again? I'll let you all down. What if I let Tiffany down? She's been so fantastic lately – and she's been so brave about the noseband."

"Just do your best," said Katy, patting Bean's arm.

"You looked great at the last practice," said Dee-Dee.

"Oh, why couldn't you do the dressage?" whimpered Bean. "Dolly would just walk it."

"OK, you go to shows with my mum," offered Dee. Bean pulled a face at her. Suddenly the dressage didn't seem so bad after all.

"Just do your best, that's all we ask," said James. "No-one is going to blame you if you don't do well."

"Oh, my legs are shaking so much, I don't think I can mount Tiffany," moaned Bean.

We all shoved her into the saddle and I glanced at Tiffany. "Don't worry," she said, huffily, "I'm going for it this time." She gulped. "Is it time for the noseband?"

As we threaded the noseband on at the very last minute, Tiffany closed her eyes and swallowed hard. She really did hate it. I had to admire her courage – but could she get past her bad memories? And could Bean remember the test?

Tiffany pulled out all the stops and did a reasonable test with only half a head shake. Bean managed to hold it together through a few wobbly moments when we could see she wasn't sure whether to make a transition or turn across the arena. She still went wrong, though. Twice.

When Bean finished her test, we crowded round her making encouraging noises.

"Why am I so rubbish at dressage?" she cried, dismounting and ripping off the noseband before giving Tiffany some Polos. Tiffany rubbed her nose across Bean's shoulder as if to rub away the memory of the hated noseband. "I was so much better at home – I just can't remember anything when it's a competition."

Their score was forty-one percent – better but still pants. No-one else had a score less than fifty-seven percent. Gloomily, we all regrouped at a tree we'd picked out. Although there was a breeze, the sun was strong, and we tied the ponies up to some string we'd fastened around the trunk and had a break.

"My mum should be along any minute," James said, looking at his watch. "She's bringing some lunch."

Now my part was over, I was ravenous and I'd been eyeing up the burger van. I wondered what James's mum would be like. When I'd first moved to Laurel Farm, James's scruffy appearance had so fired my imagination, I'd believed him to be the son of an impoverished lord or a gypsy king. After hearing that his parents had bought him Moth at the drop of a hat, I'd had an instant re-think. I'd seen his dad – he often dropped James off at the stables in his (quite expensive-looking) car, but I'd yet to meet his mum.

Petite, blonde, expensively dressed, James's mum looked chic, young and very, very glamorous, like an ex-model or something. James ran to help her carry the huge coolbox she had brought along, and she opened it up and invited us all to dig in. There were sandwiches, sausage rolls, scotch eggs and crisps, then éclairs, doughnuts, cheesecakes – and cans of Coke and Fanta underneath. Dee-Dee, Bean and I stuffed ourselves, and Katy and James made us hold some back for them to eat later – they were feeling too nervous to tackle anything now.

"I'll only bring it back up again," Katy told us.

"Yuk, don't waste it!" Bean exclaimed, cramming another doughnut into her mouth, happier now her part in the Challenge was over.

"Oh, James," I yelled, "you've only got ten minutes to warm up!"

Tightening his girth, James leapt into Moth's saddle and headed for the show jumping ring at a fast trot.

Katy volunteered to stay with the ponies, so the rest of us, together with James's mum, followed him over. As we walked across the grass, James's mum fell in step with me.

"James thinks very highly of you, Pia. He says you've helped him a lot with Moth," she said, smiling.

"Oh, well, I hope so," I muttered. I could feel myself going red. How wonderful that James thought highly of me. I felt like I was walking on air.

India Hammond was in the collecting ring on the Dweeb and talking to a girl with glasses on a piebald pony. Bean and Dee-Dee went to help adjust poles for James and Moth to practise over, and as James's mum and I stood anxiously waiting for James to jump, I could hear the Dweeb and the piebald pony talking.

"How's it goin', then?" the piebald asked in a northern accent. I remembered that I had promised myself to do some research into whether ponies had regional accents – and this seemed to confirm it.

"Well, I find this all a bit – forgive me – provincial," said the Dweeb. She sounded quite posh and a bit up herself.

"Whaddya mean?" said the piebald, not posh at all.

"Oh you know, it's not quite what I'm used to. I

mean, when one has jumped at the NEC this smacks rather of, well, to be frank, pot-hunting."

"Oh, a bit beneath you is it, this?"

"Quite! If I don't get a clear here I might as well retire! Of course, the NEC was in my younger days, and I'm not sure India even knows how good I really am. I changed homes so many times – as talented ponies do, you know. My name was Platinum Bell then. Ahhh, wonderful times," she sighed.

"That must be a right big burden t'yer," the piebald said, sarcastically.

You know when you hear a snippet of information you know to be important but you can't really unravel its significance at the time? I got that feeling when I heard the Dweeb, so I filed it away for future reference. I couldn't do much else right then because James and Moth galloped into the ring, grabbing all my attention.

"Oh, come on James," breathed his mum, crossing her fingers on both hands. Bean and Dee-Dee scooted up behind us and we all held our collective breaths. Moth looked fired up and ready for action. The pair of them flew round like they were late for an appointment – which is how Moth always tackles jumps – and only one flimsy pole dropped on a nasty upright, giving her a ten second penalty.

We all leapt in the air and screamed, "Well done, James!"

We grinned at one another. The ponies were being just ace this time!

We followed James and a puffing Moth back to the tree and gave Katy the great news.

"Fantastic!" she cried. Then her face dropped. "Oh, I hope I'm not going to spoil it all."

"Don't be silly," I told her. "Bluey is our anchor pony!"

It really did seem that we were invincible this time. We could easily drop Bean's score and still do well at this rate. I couldn't wait to see Catriona's face when she found out how improved we were.

We had at least half-an-hour before Bluey was scheduled to go cross-country and it was when I was munching on yet another of James's mum's sausage rolls that my thoughts returned to what I'd overheard the Dweeb tell the piebald. Because I thought I remembered reading in the rules that this competition was restricted to ponies who were not competing at national level. It was strictly not allowed to have any team members who had jumped under BSJA rules. If the Dweeb had indeed been to the NEC – and that had to mean she had competed at either the Horse of the

Year Show or the British Open – then she wasn't eligible to compete in the Sublime Equine Challenge. End of! My mind rambled on and reached an inevitable conclusion: the Dweeb's experience meant that Cat and Leanne's team was breaking the rules.

Cheating.

But then, just as that nasty word popped into my head, another, worse thought followed it – was I cheating, too? Because there was no doubt about it, Epona had allowed me to listen to the ponies on my team, and it had dramatically improved our performance. If I hadn't heard them, would we still be struggling?

My head hurt.

I had to share this.

As Katy rode off on Bluey (with Bluey getting excited at the prospect of doing his favourite thing), I collared James and Bean.

"I've got something to tell you both," I told them. "I need your opinions."

"OK, let's have it," said James, between bites of an éclair. Cream oozed out and dripped on to his blue tie. I ignored it.

"You know the Dweeb?" I said.

"India's pony," said Bean, on the ball for once.

"Well, according to the rules, I think she's overqualified to be in this event."

James gave a low whistle. More cream spluttered out.

"Oh, pur-leese!" wailed Bean, flicking bits of second-hand cream off her jacket.

"I overheard her saying she'd jumped at the NEC," I continued.

"So?" said Bean.

I knew her focus wouldn't last.

"This competition is for ponies which have never competed under rules."

"The cheats!" Bean exclaimed, looking round wildly for the secretary's tent. "Let's tell on them, get them disqualified."

"Hold on . . ." I said, grabbing her arm, "I'm worried they might have something on us, too."

"Like what?" James said, indignantly. "We're not cheating."

"No?"

"Get to the point, Pia!" Bean cried.

"Well, what about my little talk to the ponies? How can we explain our remarkable improvement? Cat and Leanne know about my pony whisperer status, they could kick up about that, too!"

"Mmmm, tricky," said James, stroking his chin.

Why do boys do that? "But they don't know about your chat with the ponies."

"They're cheating!" wailed Bean. "It's not fair!"

"I'm not sure they even know they're breaking the rules," I said.

"You're kidding!" exploded James. "How can they not know?"

"The Dweeb was called something else then, it was a long time ago. I don't think India is even aware of her history."

"Well, we still have to say something. We still have to get them eliminated," Bean said.

"They'll want to know how we know," murmured James.

"Exactly!" I said, thankful someone else appreciated the problem.

"Oh!" said Bean. Her forehead went all corrugated as she worked it all out in her mind. Then, once she had, she shrugged her shoulders and sighed. "So we're stuck with it?"

"It rather looks that way," I said, thinking that things would have been simpler if I hadn't overheard the Dweeb's conversation. Epona wasn't always a blessing.

The loudspeaker announced the departure of Katy and Bluey as they galloped towards the first fence on the cross-country and we watched as Bluey's black-and-grey speckled backside disappeared into the distance.

"God, wouldn't it be awful if Bluey made a hash-up of it," said Bean, chewing her nails.

"Shhhh, don't say that!" I said.

Bluey didn't make a hash-up. He romped home after a fabulous round and we all jumped up and down, hugging one another.

The Great Eight finished third behind the professional-looking team of chestnuts and a team of three boys and a girl who looked like they'd been doing this all their lives. We were soooo made up – and a bit stunned!

"We'll have to get your mum to come along next time, too," said Bean. "She's our good-luck charm."

"And if she brings some more food, that'll be ace!" I agreed.

"Yes, you greedy lot," interrupted Katy, "I never did get any of that. Any left?"

"No chance!" laughed James.

We made a huge fuss of the ponies.

"Well, we kept our word," said Drummer.

"You were brilliant!" I told him, keeping ours. I hugged his neck, planting a huge kiss on his cheek.

"Awww, get off!" he mumbled.

"But do you realise the best bit?" James said.

"What?" said Katy, rummaging around the coolbox for crumbs.

"Team SLIC had a disastrous time of it – poor Warrior got bitten by a horsefly as he was doing his cross-country round and went ballistic, which meant Scott had to retire. That means we've each got one qualifier under our belts, and both teams need to finish in the first three next time to qualify. With any luck, if the next qualifier turns out like this one, we shan't have to worry about the Dweeb's secret, after all!"

"What secret?" asked Katy.

"Oh, we'll fill you in on the way home," Bean said, as we got ready to go and get our rosettes.

As we rode over to the main ring I looked towards the horsebox line. Leanne and Cat were staring at us, and they looked anything but happy. I pushed any negative thoughts to the back of my mind. I wanted to enjoy the feeling of success for a while longer and we revelled in it as we hacked home. Even the ponies picked up the mood and were in high spirits. For me, it lasted until I got back to our house.

Chapter Nine

You see, it was like this: Mum's nightmare chum Carol was visiting and they were jawing for England. OK, so Mum asked me about how the Challenge had gone. She made all the right 'Oh I'm delighted for you, Pia,' noises for, like, one minute, and then she swooped in with Brian updates, and took it from there. Because she'd been to London for the day with him. And where they hadn't been and what they hadn't seen!

They'd started off in Covent Garden, she told us both, and had coffee watching the street entertainers. Then they'd walked around St James's Park and fed the squirrels. Then they'd had lunch somewhere posh, with wine and everything – even though my mum gets a bit lairy when she's had a drink. Then Brian insisted they went to the Tate Modern to look at the weird art, only Mum said she couldn't get her head round it and Brian had tut-tutted a lot. Mum giggled as she told us she'd spent five minutes nodding sagely at an exhibit before realising it was a radiator (Carol screamed with laugher at this point). And then they'd caught the train home where, apparently, there was snogging. I so didn't want to go there – gross squared!

"I can't wait to meet him, your Brian," said Carol, helping herself to a biscuit. I couldn't wait for her to meet him, either. I didn't think Carol would take to him at all. She liked them a little wilder than cotton-wool-hair Brian.

"He's so nice," raved Mum. "He complimented me on the dress I wore today . . ."

"Oooo, that's good. This one?" Carol interrupted, peering at Mum's dress.

"Yes, he said it made a change to see a woman wearing something feminine," Mum continued. "Brian said that he likes to see a woman in a dress."

Oh, did he, I thought.

"And he said it made a nice change to be seen with someone who takes pride in their appearance," said Mum, a bit smugly.

"Oh, not so good. It sounds like he's training you," said Carol, helping herself to another biscuit. "That's typical talk for someone who wants to dissuade you from wearing trousers."

I thought so, too. Brian sounded well creepy.

"Oh, Carol, you're reading too much into it!" laughed Mum.

"Did he say anything else?"

"Well, he wouldn't let me go halves with the lunch bill. And he said he liked my hair up, and that I should always wear it like that."

"See!" exploded Carol. "He is training you!"

"It was just a compliment!" laughed Mum.

"Just watch him," Carol said, darkly, brushing crumbs off her ample chest. "He sounds manipulative to me."

And to me, I thought, without saying anything. That was a first, Carol and me agreeing on something. Usually, she's the one egging Mum on and throwing caution to the wind. It seemed she had her doubts about Brian, and so did I. But then, I wondered, would I always have doubts about Mum's boyfriends, simply because they weren't my dad? I imagined the future with Brian and Mum as an item. Not attractive. I went to bed, leaving Mum and Carol giggling over a bottle of wine. Honestly!

The next day at the yard, James rounded up the human members of the Great Eight for a meeting in the tackroom.

"What are we meeting about?" asked Bean, yawning.

"I just thought we ought to formulate our action plan for the next qualifier," James explained.

"Aren't we just trying our best to win?" said Bean. "Or is that too obvious?"

"OK, no need to be like that," said James.

"Sorry, but the farrier's due any minute and I haven't got Tiff in from the field yet. You know what Dave's like if he has to wait around."

"Yeah, but he doesn't mind if he's late," moaned Katy. "I waited over two hours for him once, and he didn't even apologise when he finally turned up, AND he spent another half-an-hour on his mobile, booking in other people."

"Is he any good, only Drummer's farrier keeps moaning about having to drive too far to shoe him. I might ask Dave to do him," I said.

"Can we concentrate on our action plan?" James interrupted. We all looked at him and remembered why we were there.

"Well, what do you suggest?" said Katy.

"How about we all watch each other as we practise, and offer any advice? I mean, eyes on the ground are valuable, and we could really improve with some constructive criticism."

"I wouldn't like to comment on Bluey," I said, shaking my head. "As I see it, he and Katy are stars and don't need any help."

"I agree," said Bean, looking at her watch.

"Well, I could do with some help," said James.

"OK, we'll all watch you," said Bean, getting up to go. "Oh no!" she exclaimed.

"What?" we all swivelled around to see.

"Twiddles-scissor-paws is sitting on my tackbox. I can't get my headcollar."

"Are you going to let a fluffy little pussy-wussy cat stop you?" grinned James.

Twiddles is one of Mrs Collin's cats. A fat tabby and a great mouser he's all purry and nice-as-pie with Mrs C, but morphs instantly into Devil Cat with everyone else. He scratches, he hisses, he doubles in size and fluffs up like a puffball cat if you so much as speak to him. Everyone's terrified of him and if Twiddles chooses to sit on anything of yours well, unlucky you, is all I can say. Bean wasn't over-reacting at seeing Twiddles all tucked-up and comfortable on her tackbox.

"You chance it if you think he's just a pussy-wussy!" said Bean. "Katy, can I borrow your headcollar?"

"Yeah, of course," Katy agreed. "Come on James, Pia and I will watch you jump Moth and make suggestions."

So Tiffany spent the next hour tied up in Bluey's purple headcollar having a pedicure, and Katy and I watched James take Moth around the jumps in the outdoor school. She thundered around, her hooves drumming on the sand surface, snorting through her nose in her usual dragon-fashion. Only we didn't do much watching, as we were too busy humping jumps and wings around, altering the height of poles and re-arranging the course to James's liking. Moth was still taking the odd pole off with her hind legs – worryingly.

"You know what, Pia?" Katy puffed, struggling to push a jump cup through a hole in the wing. "We have so been set up."

"How?" I asked, hauling a pole around.

"Hey, James!" Katy shouted. "You just wanted us here to alter the course for you, didn't you?"

James grinned. "No, I need your advice. Honest!" he yelled, aiming Moth for the double and leaning forward as Moth launched herself into the air. She really was an exuberant jumper.

"Oh, that's a dirty trick!" I yelled, dropping the pole in disgust.

"You're still helping, I can practise much more if I don't have to keep getting off to move stuff around. It's for the team!" James said, cunningly.

"You ride with awfully long stirrups, James," observed Katy.

"Yeah, what of it?" James said, pulling up Moth for a breather.

"Well, I always shorten my stirrups at least two holes when I go cross-country," Katy said, thoughtfully. "Perhaps your stirrup length is making Moth drop her hind legs too early. You're not able to stay off her back."

I looked at Katy, then at James. His stirrups *were* very long. Everyone knows you need shorter stirrups for jumping, but somehow this information had passed James by.

"I'll give it a go," said James, adjusting his stirrups there and then.

"Wow!" I exclaimed, as James and Moth cleared all the jumps in fine style. "It's like magic!"

"Yeah, well, we could do with a bit of magic to help us," said Katy. James caught my eye – little did Katy know that any success we'd had so far had relied heavily on some magic from a certain 2000-year-old stone artefact.

Epona!

Chapter Ten

"I've got it!" cried Dee, handing out ice lollies. She'd stopped off at the village shop on her way to the yard and bought everyone a Mini-milk. Soon, all that could be heard in the tackroom was the sound of slurping. It was a great idea because it was really, really hot. The tackroom, however, was really, really cool, which made it the location of choice on a hot day.

"Got what?" said Bean, lifting her lolly up and out of reach of Mrs Collins's greyhound, Squish, who had suddenly become everyone's friend.

"An idea on how we can make sure we qualify for Hickstead," Dee said.

"Well, don't keep it to yourself," I slurped.

"My granddad. He can help us."

Katy, Bean and I looked at her blankly. James hadn't arrived yet but he was due any moment as he had another jumping practice planned.

"Is he one of the dressage judges?" Bean asked hopefully, twirling her long blonde hair up on top of her head to keep cool.

"No, he's dead."

We all stopped mid-slurp. We hadn't seen that one coming.

"Er, sorry, I'm missing something," said Katy. "Get lost, Squish, I don't hang around when you're eating your bits of dead cow!"

"We can call up his dear-departed spirit."

"Oh, of course, we've been so stupid!" I said, slapping my forehead dramatically. "What are you on, Dee?"

"No, honest, it will work, I've done it before," she said earnestly. "We use a ouija board and ask for his help. He used to be a wiz with horses when he was alive. Really good with them – rode at all the top shows. That's why my mum's so horsey, he died before I was born. He'll help us."

"Your mum's horsey because your granddad died before you were born?" asked Bean, confused.

"No, because he was!" sighed Dee, like we were strange.

"He was what?" Katy asked.

"Horsey!"

"And you want us to call up his ghost?" Bean said slowly. For once, she wasn't the only one having trouble.

"Yes, of course!"

"And you've done it before?" Katy asked.

"Yes!"

"Gross!" exclaimed Bean.

"How can that help?" I said, finishing my Mini-milk with a flourish and throwing the stick into the rubbish sack.

"I don't know, but I called him up with my cousin once, when she wanted help with her exams, and she passed with fantastic grades. Granddad helped her."

"How do you know?" said Katy.

"Because she was rubbish at all her subjects."

At that moment, James arrived, and Dee gushed out her bonkers plan again. But James was dead keen – and he wasn't just joking.

"Great idea!" he enthused. "Is that lolly for me?"

It was, but when James tore open the wrapper, the Mini-milk – morphed by the heat into creamy gunge – oozed out all over the floor, so Squish got lucky after all.

We decided that we had nothing to lose by giving

Dee's idea a try so an argument followed about what to use for a ouija board. According to Dee, we needed to write all the letters of the alphabet on the board so that her granddad could spell out words of wisdom for us with a glass, which we would place, upside down, on the board. There was simply nothing around we could use as the board. Then Katy had an idea.

"How about a tackbox? We can draw letters on the bottom," she suggested.

Everyone had a tackbox where they kept all sorts of stuff: grooming kit, treats, spare bandages. Katy's was big with purple hearts drawn all over it (who'd have guessed it!); Bean's had a broken lock and was full of very old, very tatty, half-clean stuff (she's not very tidy). Pictures of Tiffany were stuck all over it, only they were curling up with the damp, making the box look even more disreputable. Mine was painted white and I'd written DRUMMER across it. James had a filing cabinet his dad had thrown out, which was huge. Ironically, it had the least in it.

"Who's?" I said. I didn't fancy Dee's granddad going to work on the bottom of my tackbox. Actually, I didn't like the whole idea much at all.

We all looked at one another. No-one volunteered a tackbox.

"I know," said James, taking a look down the drive to make sure there was no-one about, "we'll borrow Mrs Bradley's. She won't even know."

Seizing Mrs Bradley's small and compact tackbox from under Henry's saddle rack, he flipped it upside down. You know those toy boxes that make a moo-ing or baaa-ing sound when you turn them over? Mrs B's tackbox did a similar thing, only the sound it made was all her stuff tumbling from the bottom to the top. Anxious glances were exchanged.

"What makes you think she won't know?" said Bean, chewing her lip.

"Stop worrying!" said James, breezily. "What do we do now, Dee?"

"You need to write the alphabet on it," said Dee, handing James the chalk from the blackboard where everyone left notes to one another like, *Katy, can you turn out Tiff on Tuesday, please, Bean.*

James wrote the letters A to Z all around the box in a rather crammed circle. I pulled a face at Bean – I could tell by the way she wrinkled up her nose that she wasn't very keen on this idea either.

"Now we need a glass," Dee said.

"That's a no-no," said Katy. "Will this beaker do?"

"It will have to. Come on, we all have to sit around

the board and put a finger on the glass, I mean beaker."
Dee turned the beaker upside down and placed it in
the centre of the tackbox.

"Close the door," hissed James, sitting down on an
upturned bucket. Katy shoved Squish out and pulled
the tackroom door shut. There wasn't much light –
the window was full of cobwebs, but Dee said the
gloom would give the spirits confidence to come to
us. It didn't do my confidence any good. Then we
all sat around the board and gingerly put our fingers
on the beaker.

"Just lightly – don't press down too hard," instructed
Dee. "Granddad's spirit goes inside the beaker and
moves it around to spell out a message."

Bean snatched her hand back into her chest. "I really
don't like this . . ." she said, shivering.

"Oh Bean, don't be such a fairy," scoffed James,
grabbing her hand and forcing her finger back on to
the beaker. "Come on Dee, call up gramps!"

I wasn't keen either, but not wanting to look a wuss I
gingerly put my finger on the beaker and hoped nothing
would happen. I hoped Mrs Bradley wouldn't suddenly
appear at the door, too. Try explaining that one, I thought.
And I couldn't imagine Mrs Collins being thrilled about
us holding a seance in her tackroom, either.

"Is there anybody there?" Dee murmured, slowly and dramatically.

Katy snorted, trying not to laugh.

"Shhhh!" hissed Dee. "Is there anybody there?" she said, over and over again.

I started to relax. Nothing was happening – nothing was going to happen. I felt a bit stupid for feeling scared. Then, just as I was starting to get bored, the beaker moved.

"Ahhhh!" screamed Bean, Katy and I collectively, snatching away our hands with lightning speed. The beaker went flying and I could feel my heart thudding in my chest.

"Oh, you've ruined it – we were just getting somewhere!" wailed Dee.

"Come on, let's try again. And DON'T OVERREACT!" instructed James, sternly.

"You pulled back, too!" I pointed out.

"Yeah, well, I wasn't expecting it," James said, shrugging his shoulders.

Dee did her *Is there anybody there?* bit again, and the beaker moved again, to collective gasps.

"Who is it? Who is there?" asked Dee.

The beaker started moving towards the letters, slowly at first, then faster.

"a . . . d . . . a . . . m . . . r . . ." spelled out Dee.

"James, you're moving it!" accused Katy.

"I am not!" hissed back James.

"Who is then?" whispered Katy.

"Shut up!" Dee hissed. "o . . . w . . . e . . ."

"Adam Rowe," said James. "He's moving it."

"Are you Adam Rowe?" said Dee.

"He just said he is," whimpered Bean.

"Or was!" said James, dramatically.

"Is that your granddad?" I asked Dee. She shook her head.

I felt a shiver run up and down my spine. I was liking this less and less by the minute. Who had we called up here?

"Do you have a message for us?" said Dee, completely unphased.

"Ask him whether he can help us win the Challenge," whispered Katy. "Or ask him whether he knows your granddad."

The beaker started moving around the board, spelling out a message.

"b . . . a . . . d . . . d . . . e . . . a . . . t . . . h . . . b . . . a . . . d . . . d . . . e . . . a . . . t . . ."

"I really don't like this!" moaned Bean, biting the nails on her free hand.

"Sorry to hear about your bad death," said James, rather irreverently, "but we have a pressing need to talk to Dee's granddad. Can you put him on, please?"

I gulped. This was totally getting out of hand. I mean, what if the bad death wasn't about the spirit we'd called up. What if . . . ?

"We need help with the next stage of the Sublime Equine Challenge," said Dee, staying focused. "We need your help, Granddad. We know you had a special way with horses. Can you help us?"

The beaker stopped. Then it shuffled about a bit and started on its journey again.

"b . . . a . . . d . . ."

"Oh not again," grumbled James. The beaker stopped. Then started again.

"h . . . a . . . v . . . e . . . f . . . a . . . i . . . t . . . h . . ."

"Someone IS pushing it. Who is it?" demanded Katy – only because she was whispering, she didn't sound very demanding. "OK, if that's really a spirit, prove it!" she continued.

"Oh, don't, you'll make it cross," wailed Bean, as the beaker went faster and faster in demented circles, not spelling anything at all.

"If you are a spirit, then make Squish bark!"

challenged Katy, which was clever of her because Squish never barks.

Only at that precise moment, HE DID. No, really, he did, exactly then!

Not surprisingly, pandemonium broke out in the following order:

1. Everybody screamed.

2. Scrambling to our feet we burst out of the tackroom, pushing one another aside in our best disaster movie impression.

3. Because of our undignified exit, Mrs Bradley's tackbox defied gravity and flew up towards the ceiling.

4. We were all out in the sunshine by the time the tackbox hit the floor with an almighty crash.

Bean wailed like one of the cats, I couldn't stop myself from shuddering and Katy was as white as a sheet. James was bent over double, he was laughing so much. Dee just looked cross.

"You ruined it!" she moaned to Katy.

"Me? What did I do?"

"Ooooh, I never want to do that again!" groaned Bean, wrapping her arms around in a self-hug. I agreed with her.

"That was so not a good idea, Dee!" I muttered.

Katy gave James a shove. "You were so pushing that

beaker, James. I know it was you!"

Whether she really thought so, or whether she wanted to believe it was James spelling out the words, we couldn't tell. I know I wanted to believe James was responsible.

"I couldn't make Squish bark, though, could I?" said James, grinning at her. I didn't want to think of that – it was just too creepy.

We sent James back in to return Mrs Bradley's tackbox to its rightful place. We were all too freaked to have anything more to do with it.

"So Granddad said to have faith," mused Dee, tapping her chin with her finger and looking thoughtful.

"Oh Dee, you don't really think that was your granddad, do you?" I asked.

"Oh course, I told you, he's helped out before. Just you wait and see!" she said, nodding. "Now Granddad's on board, you'll all walk the next qualifier, you just see if you don't!"

It wasn't until later when I was de-cobwebbing Drummer's stable from a distance, with a broom (which takes me ages 'cos if I see a spider, I have to run out of the stable until it's gone), and my thoughts were rambling along like they do, when I wondered whether

I could summon up the spirits to do something about Skinny Lynny. Like make her disappear. Or go off my dad, or diet away to nothing – or at the very least, never want to go riding again. Or could I influence my dad and get him back together with my mum? And if I could, would Mum want that? Would I?

And then my thoughts meandered on to considering whether I could make Brian less of a nerd, or even make him go away altogether. Perhaps he could join the navy, or get posted to Scotland (poor Scotland!) or get lost on a school trip in the Welsh mountains. But just as I had Brian stuck down a hole on the Brecon Beacons, calling for help, with no-one within earshot, a spider dropped down too close for comfort and forced me outside.

In the sun, I realised I was getting really carried away with this spirit lark. How easy it is for evil to take a hold, I thought. I really had to get a grip. Mum says it's seriously bad karma to wish ill on other people (she usually says it after a mega moaning session about Skinny Lynny), and that it will only come back on you two-fold. So then I got to wondering whether I would try the ouija board thing out on Skinny and Brian if karma wasn't the only thing stopping me; and whether karma and conscience were the same thing; and in the end my head started to feel a bit full up with so many thoughts, so I took Drummer for a ride and let the dust settle in his stable and my brain.

When I got into bed that night, and started imagining all sorts of things – mainly when I heard a floorboard squeak or could hear all the usual night sounds which seemed suddenly spooky – I totally wished we hadn't let Dee talk us into the ouija board thing. I made up my mind I was never, ever going to do it again.

Chapter Eleven

The third qualifier was make-or-break time. If we didn't come in the first three placings here, it was bye-bye Hickstead dream. I couldn't help wondering whether Dee's granddad really was looking down on us (or up. I mean, how could we tell?).

It took us ages to hack over to Lambourne Farm, which is quite a posh equestrian centre on top of a hill. It was a hot day, so we got there early so the ponies could rest before the classes. The dressage was held in the massive indoor school. Tiffany and Bean were due in directly after a particularly good test by a grey pony ridden by a very tall girl who sniffed all the way round.

"Why doesn't she blow her nose?" hissed Bean.

"Perhaps it's a habit," I hissed back. "Can you remember the test?"

"Don't ask!" she said. "And don't put me under

pressure, for goodness' sake!"

Tiffany and Bean performed in their usual fashion – two missed transitions, one wobble when Bean was undecided about a circle or a turn and one stop-dead-and-check-out-the-letters-before-proceeding-with-caution. Her score was thirty-nine. What could we say? Bean had warned us how it would be. Outside the arena, Tiffany rubbed her nose on a front leg to get rid of the feel of the noseband.

"You think it would get easier," she said to me, "but actually, it's worse each time."

"We all appreciate your bravery, Tiff," I told her, patting her snowy mane.

"Still rubbish, though. You all have to pull your hooves out," Tiff told Drummer and Moth. "I'm done for the day! I don't like the look of those flags, by the way. Very nasty."

Our ace, Bluey, completed his customary fast clear. He was like a machine. We sponged him down with some cool water as Katy slithered out of the saddle and thanked him. Scott and Warrior thundered round with no penalties whatsoever and looked like it would have taken a natural disaster to stop them, or even slow them down.

"I wish we'd had a big fat horsefly on our side

today," sighed Bean, obviously not the slightest bit worried by karma.

"We only have to come third to qualify," James reminded us.

Drum gave his best performance yet ("The sooner it's over, the sooner I can get out of this ridiculous costume!" were his exact words) and we got a high score from the judges. I didn't see Cat and Bambi's performance as they had been the first to go. From the scoreboard, I could see they had a good score – better than mine.

"No pressure, James," remarked Bean, "but it's all up to you, now!"

"Piece of cake!" said James. But he pulled a face to show he wasn't taking anything for granted. Since altering his stirrups, Moth had hardly touched a pole and although he and Moth had a nasty moment at a tricky oxer, and Moth slipped going into the stile, causing us all to hold our breath, nothing fell and we all leapt up and down and squealed like boyband fans when James rode out with a clear round and no penalties. The Great Eight were on the up!

"See," said Dee, "I said my granddad would help us."

"I don't see why he should take all the credit," said James.

"He didn't help me much," grumbled Bean, "it took me ages to get to sleep that night. I kept imagining all sorts of things whenever I heard a squeak or a thump. It was a lousy idea."

I was glad I hadn't been the only one who'd imagined things when I'd gone to bed. I didn't think it worth mentioning.

India was next to jump on the Dweeb. As she cantered into the ring, we had a bit of a pow-wow.

"Is that the pony who's overqualified?" Katy whispered to me.

"Yes. She was called Platinum Bell when she jumped at the NEC."

"It doesn't make sense," said Dee. "Well-known ponies command a higher price, so why would anyone want to keep it a secret? I can't believe India doesn't know her pony is so experienced."

"Maybe there's a reason for it," suggested Bean. The bell went, and India headed the Dweeb, aka Platinum Bell, towards the first jump.

"What kind of reason?" I said.

"I don't know. Perhaps India stole her," Bean suggested wildly.

India and the Dweeb cleared the first jump and cantered neatly towards the next. I couldn't get the image of India, in cartoon burglar garb of a black-and-white striped top and black mask, unbolting the Dweeb's stable and leading her away in the dead of night. No, that couldn't be it.

"Or," said James, "perhaps she's a pot-hunter who likes winning at local shows on a pony who can blow the opposition away."

Tucking up her forelegs neatly, the Dweeb cleared the stile with masses to spare.

I looked at James. "Are you serious?"

"I don't know," he shrugged. "I'm just clutching at straws. India doesn't seem the sort to pull a fast one. She's rather nice."

Twang went my heart. James thought India was rather nice.

"I know," agreed Katy, "I can't believe she knows about her pony's past."

The pony who had told the piebald that she thought these qualifiers a bit 'provincial' got it all wrong at the next and dropped her hind legs on to the pole, knocking it off and collecting ten penalties.

"Woohoo!" yelled Bean, immediately clapping her hand over her mouth and turning bright red. "Oh dear, I so didn't mean to say that out loud. Sorry."

Several people nearby tut-tutted, so we crept away,

trying to look ashamed.

A team of two chestnuts, an Appaloosa and a bay won the qualifier, ridden by three sisters and their cousin. They had a big horsebox and looked very serious about it all. Cat and Leanne's team was second, and we went wild when the loudspeaker announced that the Great Eight had taken third place.

Two third places. We'd qualified!

"I don't believe it, we're going to Hickstead!" shouted Katy, hanging around Bluey's neck and smothering him with kisses. Bluey looked pleased in a pleased-pony sort of way.

Bean did a dance on the spot, causing Tiffany to stick her head in the air and run backwards.

"Hear that Moth? We're off to the big-time!" James said.

Moth said nothing.

"Drummer, you're going to Hickstead, what do you think of that?" I told Drum.

"Do I have to wear those ear things, there?" Drum replied.

"Oh, I so wish I was in the team. It's not fair!" wailed Dee.

"But you're always riding Dolly at all the top shows!" Katy reminded her.

"It's not the same, really it isn't," moaned Dee.

I couldn't believe we were going. We really were going.

To Hickstead.

I imagined riding around the famous arena, bumping into show jumpers, being applauded in the main ring. Awesome!

We hastily smartened ourselves up so we wouldn't look too shabby next to the horsebox-sister-cousin combo, and were excitedly waiting to go into the main arena to collect our rosettes when the loudspeaker crackled into action again, informing everyone that an objection had been lodged. And that it needed to be cleared before the placings could be recorded. It boomed out across the showground to tell everyone that the objection was against a member of the Great Eight.

Pia Edwards.

Me.

Chapter Twelve

I gulped. What had I done? Had I broken the rules? If so, how? Which bit of kit had I left off Drum? Thoughts raced around my head but I couldn't imagine what the objection could be about.

"It's your wretched granddad," Bean hissed to Dee. "I bet it's against the rules to get help from dead relations."

"Who would know?" mumbled Dee, guiltily.

"You should let dead granddads lie," Katy told her.

"What could be the reason, Pia?" James asked and I shook my head and shrugged my shoulders. How could I know?

"I'll come with you, let's go," he said, grimly, and leaving Drum and Moth with the others, we made our way to the secretary's tent. And guess who was there with two of the organisers – a woman in glasses and a man in a tweed coat – Cat and Leanne. My heart sank. If Cat was behind this, it had to be bad. James said who we were and the woman looked all flustered at me over her glasses.

"I'm Julia Williams and this is Robert Best, we're two of the judges for this Sublime Equine Challenge."

We knew that. They both wore name badges under another, enamel badge which said JUDGE.

"What seems to be the problem?" James asked, briskly.

My throat seemed to have dried up and I didn't trust myself to speak. I felt guilty, even though I was sure I hadn't done anything wrong.

Julia Williams turned to Cat, "Er, well, this young lady seems to think your team mate has an unfair advantage," she explained.

"You know what I'm talking about," cried Cat, lifting her chin defiantly. Leanne looked a bit uncomfortable.

"No, I don't," I croaked. Because I didn't.

"You're a pony whisperer, you can communicate with the ponies. That's how you do your Wild Card show. It isn't fair and you know it!"

I sniggered. I couldn't help it.

"It's no laughing matter, young lady," said Robert Best, sternly.

"It is!" I said, turning to Cat. "You've always said I wasn't a pony whisperer! You've always insisted that I was lying. But now it suits you, you want me to be." I could feel Epona in my jodhpur pocket and a shiver ran down my spine. They couldn't search me, could they?

"That is true, Cat," James said. Then he turned to Robert Best. "Honestly, Mr Best, Ms Williams, do you really believe that Pia here can possibly communicate with ponies? I mean, do you?" He was a cool one, James knew that I could.

Both judges looked sheepish. Clearly, they didn't believe it at all. Julia Williams coughed. "Well, we have to take all objections seriously," she said, "and Catriona here says that Pia has been on the television, with her own show."

My heart did a somersault. She had me there, I couldn't deny that. Was I going to be disqualified? If so, our team would be out, with no chance of getting to Hickstead. Cat was just being spiteful – she'd qualified for Hickstead and getting me disqualified didn't benefit her or her team at all. I couldn't understand why she was being so mean. The trouble was, Cat was right, I did have an advantage, a huge one. But then, I realised with a start, so did she. Glancing at James, I could see that the same thought had occurred to him to.

"Hey, Leanne," he said, "got a minute? Outside?"

"What? Now?"

"Oh yes, right now! Excuse us." James steered Leanne out of the tent.

"Now Catriona," said Julia Williams, "how can you possibly prove your incredible accusation?"

"Yes, Cat, how are you going to do that? Ask the ponies?" I said sarcastically.

"You're a cheat!" Cat said quietly, her green eyes blazing.

"Well, I really don't see how we can reach any kind of agreement on this," said Julia Williams.

"But the fact remains that an objection has been lodged," interrupted Robert Best. "If this girl has had her own television show, then we have to believe that she has some ability and may, with all things considered, have some advantage. We need time to investigate . . ."

Things were looking grim. Where was James? What was he doing? And why was it taking him so long?

". . . therefore, I have no choice but to uphold . . ."

"STOP!" shouted Leanne, bursting into the tent with James hot on her heels. "We've changed our minds, we don't want to lodge an objection after all."

"WHAT!" screamed Cat, totally losing it.

"Yes, I mean no, I mean, we honestly don't want to. Sorry but it's all been a terrible mistake. Come on, Cat, let's go."

"But Brighton's about to be thrown out!" Leanne whispered something in Catriona's ear. Cat said nothing. She just pressed her lips together, turned white and stormed out of the tent with Leanne running to catch up with her.

"That seems to be the end of the objection," said James meekly, smiling at Julia Williams and Robert Best.

"This is all very irregular," said Robert Best.

"Well, I'm glad it's all resolved," sighed Julia Williams, clearly not keen on confrontation.

Relieved, we bolted back to the others and got them up to speed.

"Good job we had our ace card up our sleeves," explained James. "If Pia hadn't overhead the Dweeb 'fessing up to the piebald job, we'd have been out for sure. It was a close one."

"But that just makes it worse," said Katy, who is very honest. "It was Pia's pony-whispering skills that allowed her to find that out in the first place, proving Cat's point. Maybe we should be disqualified."

"Oh Katy, don't be so noble!" exclaimed Bean. "Cat's team has a red-hot show jumping pony to help them. That's cheating, too. Even more so!"

"But now they go through too," Dee pointed out. "That can't be right, either!"

"Well, we'll just have to beat them fair and square at Hickstead!" said James, talking us all up.

I shuddered. It had been a narrow escape and I felt a bit shivery about it. Technically, Cat was right, I did have an advantage, a big one. But they had ace show jumper Platinum Bell on their team. If either team won the Sublime Equine Challenge, would that be right? How could we justify two wrongs – when everyone knows they don't make a right.

Whether it was wrong or right, I couldn't let the team down now. I twirled Epona around in my pocket. Ever since I'd found her she'd presented me with problems, this was just her latest. But I was in this thing now, and in too far to stop. James was right; we had to beat Catriona's team fair and square. And if we did beat them using Epona, weren't we just as bad?

Why were things always so difficult? Oh poo, poo, poo!

Chapter Thirteen

Despite the bad feeling with Leanne and Cat, I was dead excited about Drummer and me going to Hickstead. I mean, how totally fab was that? I kept grinning to myself, and jumping up and punching the air and shouting YES! to no-one at all. I couldn't wait to tell Mum all about it. But when I got home, there was a note in the kitchen to say she'd gone to some classical concert with Brian, and that she'd left me a chicken pie in the fridge. Mum always said she hated classical music, said it gave her the right hump. She always preferred modern music. She even liked some rap. I wondered whether she'd told Brian about that. It seemed Carol was right, Brian was training my mum, and music was the latest subject.

A vision of life with Brian wafted before my eyes: Brian taking up valuable space on our sofa, feet up, eyes shut, hands conducting a violin concerto. Brian in charge of the TV remote, forcing us to watch cultural programmes instead of the usual mindless rubbish we like, and asking us questions all the way through to check whether we were paying attention. Brian banging on about collective nouns and personal pronouns and being all teacher-ish ALL THE TIME! It was too unbearable for words. As I banged a plate on to the worktop and slammed the cutlery draw shut, the séance idea never seemed so appealing.

Then my mobile went. It was Dad.

"Hi, Pumpkin!" he boomed down the phone. He was always so happy these days and I realised with a pang that I couldn't remember him being like that when he'd been with us.

"Hello, Dad," I replied, glad I could tell him about Hickstead. I was dying to tell somebody! I'd sort the 'Pumpkin' thing another day.

"Oh, that's marvellous, Pia," enthused Dad, after I'd explained. "I'm very proud of you. When is it? We'll have to come and see you, especially as Lyn is having riding lessons at Stocks Hall. Her instructor says she's a natural."

What! A green film of jealousy misted over my eyes. What I wouldn't do to have lessons at Stocks Hall – I'd ride like Zara Phillips if I did! There could only be three reasons why Skinny's instructor said she was a natural:

1. The instructor was either a. blind or b. stupid (or both!).

2. He was sucking up like mad 'cos lessons at Stocks Hall cost an arm and a leg.

3. Skinny was, indeed, a natural.

Obviously, it had to be one of the first two – or possibly both.

"You'll have to go riding together," Dad went on. "How about on holiday? We could go to Greece, or Spain or a riding safari in Africa. I might even try riding myself! A holiday together would be great fun, wouldn't it, Pia?"

I decided not to go there. My brain was hijacked by the image of using the ouija board again. I had to get a grip and put that out of my mind – talk about evil taking hold!

Dad rattled on some more telling me all about how he and Skinny had been there, done that, blah, blah, and I said 'oh nice', and 'really?' and 'sounds good' in all the right places and then he rang off after reminding me of his plan for us all to go riding together. He was certainly on a mission there.

He didn't ask about Mum. He used to, in the early days when he left her for Skinny, but now he didn't seem to care. I heard myself sigh. Maybe an African safari would be cool. I wondered what the horses would be like in the bush, and whether Epona would let me hear what the zebras were saying.

The smell of burning pastry snapped me out of my thoughts, and I turned off the oven, feeling a bit sorry for myself. Dad hadn't got the relevance of my Hickstead news at all. I wanted someone to get excited with me, to scream and be all animated and tell me what a terrific, thrilling, amazing thing I'd done and how clever I'd been. I mean, that's what parents are for, aren't they? To big you up? Not bang on about their girlfriends or leave you with a frozen pie for company while they go and listen to Schubert or Chopin or whatever. Right now, I wanted it to be about me. Me, me, me!

Mum still wasn't home by the time I went to bed, so she still didn't know her daughter's stonking, amazing news. It took me ages to get to sleep because I had a right old hump – which seemed very wrong seeing as I'd qualified to go to Hickstead, if anyone was interested. Which they clearly were NOT!

The next day, I decided to sulk and keep my

Hickstead news to myself. Mum, however, couldn't wait to tell me all about her evening.

"But you always said you hated classical music," I muttered, determined to remind her.

"Yes, I know Pia, but I need to keep an open mind. New experiences are so broadening. Brian says I need to go to places I wouldn't think of going to, to open my mind to new things. He says I really ought to learn to appreciate the arts."

"Not if you don't enjoy them," I said, determined to disagree with everything Brian said.

"But Brian says I don't know whether I'll enjoy them. I need to discover that there's a whole world out there."

"OK, does that include asking whether other people have exciting news?" I hinted.

"I need to go shopping," Mum said, ignoring me. "I'll ask Carol to come with me. I need some new clothes, something more suitable for classy events. Everyone there last night was more dressed up than me. Brian says I need something long, an evening dress. I'm letting him down."

"Did he actually say that?" I said, feeling my hackles rising.

"Well, not in so many words but I did feel quite frumpy," she continued. "I could tell Brian was uncomfortable – embarrassed even, especially when we bumped into some friends of his. They all looked very elegant. Perhaps I'll try that posh boutique in the village . . . what's it called . . . Toto . . . Totum . . . Too-too?"

"The one you said was run by the old bag with the face lift?" I reminded her. "Who sells the sort of clothes you always said were over-the-top and overpriced?" I went on, rubbing it in. Honestly, what had cotton-wool hair done to my mum?

"Well, I need something, I don't want to feel like that again. Brian's taking me to an exhibition at *Splash!* – that fancy art gallery in the high street next week, and he said I'll need to look tidy. But I'm not sure I can carry off anything too swish. I'm still carrying some extra weight. Brian says I need to lose at least five pounds, and . . ."

"WHAT?" I screamed.

Mum stopped and looked at me as though she'd just remembered I was there.

"Listen to yourself!" I ranted. "Brian says this, Brian wants that, Brian thinks something else. What do *you* want, Mum? Do you really want to be with a man who makes you feel shabby? Who tells you you're fat? Who tells you what to wear? Shouldn't you be with someone who likes you because of what you are now, not what he wants to make you into?"

Mum looked stunned but I was off, I couldn't stop now.

"You were fine when you met Brian, now all you do is what he wants. Remember how you were when Dad left? You're ten times more confident now. You don't need Brian – or anyone like him. You need someone who accepts and appreciates you for yourself. Who does Brian think he is, anyway? He's so nerdy, Mum, he doesn't deserve you."

"That's enough, Pia!" Mum found her voice at last, and I realised how rude I'd been. But I'd had it up to here with Brian. My mum didn't need him. Couldn't she see it?

"I'm going to see Drummer!" I yelled, running out of the door and slamming it behind me. I was behaving badly, but I was really upset at the thought of Brian telling my mum what to do – and he'd completely overshadowed my news of qualifying for Hickstead!

By the time I got to the yard, I felt dreadful. I hate rowing with Mum. Close to tears, I found Drummer in the field, rubbing his tail on a tree.

"Oi," I said crossly, "stop that!"

"I think I've got pinworms," he grumbled.

"So not the greeting I was hoping for!"

"Well, I thought you'd want to know, so you can do something about it," he said. "You're sweetness and light this morning, what's up?"

"Family!" I said. "Ooooh, they're enough to drive you mad!"

"Skinny Lynny?" asked Drummer.

"Not this time. It's Mum. Or rather, it's her latest boyfriend. He's such a know-all and he keeps bossing her around. I can't seem to make her see what a total loser he is."

"Mmmm, love is blind," Drummer said, his gaze drifting towards Bambi, who was rolling in the dust patch by the gate.

"Are you still infatuated with her?" I asked him.

"What can I say? She's the one," he sighed.

"She hates you," I reminded him.

"We're destined to be together, Bambi just doesn't know it yet. Besides," he looked at me again, "people and ponies have to make their own mistakes. You can't stop them from taking wrong paths, it just makes them more determined to prove you wrong."

I don't know how Drummer knows so much about life and love and the universe and everything. Either he's very wise or he's just good at talking horse poo, which sounds more likely. I chewed the inside of my mouth and thought about it.

"But Brian's such a loser!" I wailed.

"Yeah, well, if that's true, your mum will see it eventually," Drum assured me. "Now, how about taking me in for a bite to eat? Something tasty, some pony cubes, maybe some sugar beet, a few handfuls of coarse mix? It must be breakfast time – and if we don't get a wiggle on, it will merge into lunchtime and I'll miss out. Come on!"

So we wandered in, and then Bean and Katy arrived and we spent the morning practising plaiting manes and tails and dreaming about winning Hickstead and galloping around the big arena, and although Mum was still seeing Brian, and Skinny was still having riding lessons at Stocks Hall, and nobody seemed impressed that I was going to Hickstead, it somehow didn't seem so bad when I was with everyone else and I had Drummer to talk to.

It didn't seem so bad at all.

Chapter Fourteen

It was James who thought of it. It was such a totally obvious thing to consider.

But nobody had.

Katy and I were doing the supportive thing for Bean who was practising her dressage schooling in the outdoor school, when James walked over to join us, his lips grimly pressed together.

"What's up?" I asked him.

"Ooooh, is it gossip?" Katy cried eagerly, jumping down from the fence.

"Where am I supposed to canter?" yelled Bean.

"Oh, let's see . . ." I looked at the dressage test sheet in my hand. "Canter a twenty-metre circle . . . at . . . A."

"What are you doing?" asked James.

"Bean's learning her final dressage test," Katy told him.

"But she's not supposed to practise the actual test," sighed James, like we had pony poo for brains. "If the judge thinks the pony's anticipating the next movement, she'll lose marks."

"Shhhh!" I hissed, shaking his sleeve. "You know that and we know that, but Bean's in such a state about remembering the test, she has to do it this way."

"Don't you say anything, James," warned Katy, putting on her menacing face. "Just let Bean do what's right for her. We'll probably have to drop her score, anyway, so what does it matter? Get on with what you came to tell us."

James took a deep breath. "Has anyone given any thought as to how we are going to get to the final at Hickstead?" he asked.

"But we've qualified," Katy said, in a voice that suggested James was being dim. "We're G-O-I-N-G!" She did a jig on the spot in glee.

"Yes, but how? How, physically, are we G-O-I-N-G? Hack all the way?"

"Oh," I said again, feeling as though someone had let the air out of my lungs. Obviously we did have pony poo for brains, otherwise we'd have thought of that. Hickstead wasn't a hackable distance.

"Mmmm, bit of an oversight, wouldn't you say?"

agreed James, running a hand through his slightly-too-long blonde hair. It has a peculiar effect on me, him doing that, but I couldn't dwell on that now.

"What's going on?" said Bean, pulling up next to us. Tiffany snorted dramatically at a snake in the sand before it turned back into a stick. We explained the crisis.

"Well, Katy's got a trailer, two of us can go in that," said Bean, being a bit free and easy with Katy's trailer. But Katy nodded in agreement.

"But what about Moth and Drummer?" asked James. "Katy's dad can't make two trips and Hickstead is miles and miles and MILES away!"

I felt my spirits dribbling out of my boots and sinking into the grass.

"We'll just have to hire a horsebox," said Bean, matter-of-factly.

"But that will cost loads," I said, chewing my lip. Me and Mum weren't even going on holiday this year, so I knew we didn't have any spare cash for horsebox hire. The entry fees for the Sublime Equine Challenge had been difficult enough to scrape together and I hadn't any pocket money left after forking out for Drummer's ear protectors and budgie bells. James's family was obviously loaded, and I could only imagine how he was going to feel when I had to let him down. But James surprised me.

"I don't think my parents will stump up any cash for me to go," he moaned. "They're helping my sister buy a flat. They've made it plain that I have to fund any shows and events I want to do with Moth this year from my allowance."

We all stood around in gloomy silence. Tiffany rubbed her nose on the fence. Katy screwed up her face, deep in thought. I could almost feel the wind whistling through my head – empty of any ideas, as usual.

"I'm going for a hack," Bean announced in a wobbly voice, obviously gutted. She rode off through the yard, her blonde plait bobbing up and down, sitting a wobble half-way along the drive as Tiffany spotted a couple of monster rabbits. I couldn't be sure Bean wasn't actually crying and I knew how she felt. It seemed so unfair that after everyone's hard work we weren't going to be able to get ourselves to the final. James, Katy and I flung ourselves down on the grass in gloom.

"We so should have thought of this," James said.

"I can't believe we've been so stupid!" I agreed, angrily wrenching the head off a daisy.

We sat wallowing in misery, trying to think up ways to get round it and failing. When Dee arrived, declaring that she had some bad news of her own, we were less than sympathetic.

"I bet it's not as bad as ours," mumbled Katy.

"You're always moaning," said James, disappointment making him unkind.

"Yes, well, it's all right for you," wailed Dee, "you can do what you like up here. You should have your mum around all the time, telling you what to do with Moth, see how you like it."

"OK, Dee, what's your bad news?" said Katy, soothingly, anxious to avoid a scene.

"It's about Hickstead . . ."

"Yeah, ditto!" I said.

". . . I can't groom for the team at the finals . . ."

"No problem, actually," interrupted Katy, testily, "because the team can't go."

"WHAT!"

"It's true," I sighed. "Half of us can't get there because . . ."

". . . the transport's too expensive," finished James, stealing the punchline. "Only two of us can go in Katy's trailer so it's all been for nothing. So you see," he went on, "it's actually all right for you, for once."

You'll never guess what Dee did. You won't, so I'll have to tell you.

She LAUGHED!

We all stared at her. I thought Katy was going to burst. James looked ready to do murder.

Dee stopped laughing and rolled her eyes skyward. "The other two can come with us," she said, like we were stupid not to have thought of it.

I felt my jaw dropping.

"Say again?" Katy said slowly.

"Yeah, we're going. That's why I can't groom for you. Mum's entered me and Dolly for a showing class there – it's a HOYS qualifier – and it's on the same day as the Challenge. Our horsebox takes four horses and we're only taking Dolly, so there will be plenty of room. I'll ask Mum now, if you like."

She poked her tongue out at James. James just looked gobsmacked. I'd never seen him lost for words.

I looked over to Sophie's huge and expensive horsebox parked next to the barn. Could we really, possibly, ever-in-a million-years, travel to Hickstead in that? We'd not just get there, we'd get there in style!

Dee's mum Sophie was completely supportive.

"Of course you must come with us," she gushed. "You've all done so well to qualify, and we're going anyway," she said in her usual, bossy tone. Which everyone forgave because she was being so generous.

So it was settled, and when Bean returned, after much whooping and jumping about, we all had a whip-round and Bean and I cycled to the village shop to get a box of chocolates for Sophie and a couple of bags of Maltesers and marshmallows for us to celebrate. We all sat and had a major, delirious scoff-fest until Bean actually turned a bit green, jumped to her feet, ran across the yard and disappeared.

We just thought she was being strange as usual, but when she wobbled back she confessed to having thrown up on the muck heap – which we put down to the emotional roller-coaster of the day. James felt the need to point out that it was a terrible waste of good Maltesers and marshmallows. But then, I thought, that was far, far better than not being able to go to Hickstead, and we all (except Bean, who shook her head and rolled her eyes at the thought) sucked another marshmallow each to that!

Chapter Fifteen

"I can't believe we're really here!" murmured Katy, looking around the famous Hickstead showground. The rest of the Great Eight nodded in agreement. It was totally awe-inspiring, competing at the same show as some of the most famous riders in the world. I could feel butterflies doing the rumba around my stomach.

We'd hit the road at six o'clock that morning. Bluey and Tiffany were cocooned in Katy's trailer – Bluey swathed in purple from poll-guard to boots, Tiffany in a more sophisticated two-tone blue ensemble. Drummer and Moth had been rugged up in their green (it's so Drum's colour!) and black respectively, ready to go in Sophie's posh horsebox. Boy was it swish! With a ramp at the side and another at the back, four stalls *and* living accommodation, Drummer had never travelled in such four-star luxury, and neither had I. I was almost as excited about travelling in that as I was about our destination.

Dolly had gone up the ramp first and it immediately became clear why Dee hated going to shows with her mum.

"Tie her up a bit shorter," Sophie had barked from the bottom of the ramp. "Oh come on, Dee, you've done it enough times!"

"Last time, you said I tied her too short!" Dee had protested.

"Sometimes, I think you do it deliberately, just to annoy!" her mum had retorted, shaking her head.

"Why doesn't she do it herself?" I'd whispered to Dee when she came back down the ramp.

"Then she wouldn't have anything to moan about," Dee had whispered back. "She's always worse on show days – nerves."

With trepidation, and hoping I wouldn't get yelled at, I'd led Drummer up the ramp and tied him next to Dolly. Dolly had been made up.

"Oooh, hello handsome. How lovely we get some quality time together at last!" she'd cooed as Drummer had sighed.

Dolly's attentions embarrass him. I keep asking him why he doesn't just roll over and fancy glam Dolly, who clearly adores him, instead of up-herself Bambi but he says that love's like that. He must like a challenge.

"Can't Moth go here?" Drum had whispered out of the corner of his mouth. I'd grinned and patted his neck.

"Sorry! We don't get to choose. Sophie's in charge."

"Oh, oh well, that's it, then." Drummer knows an immovable force when he sees it.

With Moth safely loaded, and after a couple of minutes of Sophie going on at Dee about loading tack and not forgetting this, and remembering that, and answering her mobile a couple of times (she always seems to have her ear jammed to the mobile, which is the only respite Dee gets), Dee and Sophie got in the cab and James and I climbed into the living part behind them, and we set off down the drive after Katy's trailer.

To Hickstead. Did I mention that? I could so not sit still!

Twenty teams had qualified for the Sublime Equine Challenge – which meant that the showground was teeming with ponies, riders and their supporters – and there were lots of the usual Hickstead showing and jumping classes going on at the same time. I'd never seen so many posh horseboxes and trailers in one place and all that obvious wealth made me feel like a pauper.

Having caught up with Katy's trailer on the way, Sophie parked her swish horsebox next to it, so we were all together. Katy's dad, who's all smiley and laid-back, settled down to read the paper. Katy and James went off to find the secretary and get the lowdown on where everything was situated and the times we were due in which ring, leaving me and Bean to gaze all goggle-eyed at the exciting scene around us. It was a sunny day with a faint breeze, and the smell of hotdogs and doughnuts mingled satisfyingly with the smell of horses.

"I hope we see Ellen Whitaker," said Bean, her head on a swivel, trawling for horsey celebrities.

"Oh look there's . . . em, who exactly is that?" I said, as a man in show jumping gear whizzed past us on a bicycle.

"Dunno," said Bean, "but he must be someone famous. I thought I'd brought my autograph book . . ." she muttered, clutching her jacket pockets. The only thing I had in my pocket was a 2000-year-old goddess. Epona was safety-pinned in to make sure she didn't go missing. What a disaster that would be!

"I wonder when my mum will get here," I said, looking at the huge crowds. "Are your parents coming?"

Bean did a Tiffany-type snort. "You must be joking – they'd rather pull off their own heads. Let's go and look at the Derby Bank," she said, changing the subject and breaking into a run.

I realised I'd never seen either of Bean's parents at the yard. What was the story there, I wondered? I realised that both my parents at least tried to take an interest in my hobbies. When I'd eventually told Mum about qualifying for the final, she'd been thrilled and totally excited.

The enormous Derby Bank looked like a huge, grassy, Egyptian pyramid.

Bean's mouth fell open in awe. "I can just imagine me and Tiff sliding down that," she sighed.

Yeah, right, I thought. Tiffany would freak out half a mile away from it.

The main ring was vast and all the jumps looked newly painted and familiar – the Devil's Dyke, the Irish Bank, the water jumps. I was in heaven knowing I wasn't just a spectator, but a competitor, just like my fave horsey celebs. My stomach did a sort of jig at the thought.

We wandered through the trade stands – we didn't have time to stop – and found our way back to the horsebox, bumping into Ben Maher on the way.

I say bumping – he walked by and Bean and I pulled faces at each other in excitement. It was so weird seeing people I'd only ever seen on the TV, up close and personal.

We got back to Sophie's horsebox and unloaded the ponies, stripping off rugs and travel boots and checking they were OK. Moth had rubbed out one of her plaits, so Bean sewed it back in again before James and Katy returned.

"Here, I've got our numbers. Katy's got the times and we walked the cross-country course together, so that's all done," said James, handing out the numbers.

"They've built the course specially for this event," said Katy, "and it's gorgeous. Bluey's going to love it!"

We looked at the note James held with our times written on it. James and Moth were up first, then me and Drum followed by our secret weapon, Katy and Bluey (only they weren't much of a secret), with Bean and Tiffany going last. Seeing my name in the programme prompted an excited tingle and a stab of fear. I wasn't the only one with worries.

"Oh God, I'm last and I just KNOW I'm going to forget the test and let you all down," wailed Bean.

"You won't forget it this time," I said, crossing my fingers behind me against the probability of telling a big, fat lie. "You've practised it so often at home, you'll remember it today." I didn't really believe it. Secretly, I wished Katy was going last.

James wasn't so diplomatic. "Have a day off, Bean. What if I make Moth drop her hind legs in a jump? Anyway, we can drop your score, like we always do."

"Thanks for the vote of confidence!" yelled Bean.

"Oh, enough of the negativity!" snapped Katy, sticking her fingers in her ears. "No more what-ifs, pur-leeese! Unless it's to say what if we all do fantastically well? What if we all perform brilliantly? What if we WIN? If you believe you'll do badly, you will. If you believe you'll do well, then guess what? You might just do that, instead!"

"Wow, that's telling us!" I said.

"OK, Katy, keep your hair on!" mumbled James.

"If you say so," said Bean, unconvinced.

"OK, now give me five!" Katy said, sticking her arm in the air.

We did. Katy can be well scary at times.

Our supporters began to arrive. First were James's parents, and they'd brought Katy's mum with them. They all chatted with Katy's dad, said all the right encouraging things to us, then disappeared to have something to eat and go round the trade stands, promising they'd be watching all of us. There was no sign of my mum yet – or Brian, who was coming, too. I wondered whether he'd make me do detention if I didn't win. Or he might make my mum do it, instead.

My dad and Skinny Lynny turned up, though. But you'll never guess what Skinny was wearing. Jodhpurs! I could have died of embarrassment. Who wears riding clothes at a show when they're not competing? SHE CAN'T EVEN RIDE!!!

I could see the others staring as Skinny stomped about in her leather boots and skin-tight jodhpurs and I could have died. Right there. Dead. At Hickstead. I imagined my team mates and Drummer shaking their heads as they gathered around me prostrate on the grass, saying, 'It's sad, but going at Hickstead, well, it's what Pia would have wanted, after all.'

"Hi, Pumpkin!" said Dad, kissing me out of my morbid thoughts and making me even crosser – with myself this time. When was I going to have a word with him about that?

"When are you on?" asked Skinny, making an attempt to pat Drummer, then backing off as he flattened his ears back and swished his tail at her.

"Not until this afternoon. Why are you wearing jodhpurs?" I had to ask.

"Oh, I thought I'd blend in," Skinny replied, airily, flicking back her hair.

"Don't they suit her!" said Dad, giving her a drippy smile.

As one of my parents took his trophy girlfriend shopping at the trade stands, my other parent arrived with her boyfriend – the one with the glued-on hair.

"Hello love," said Mum, kissing my cheek. She was wearing a plain shirt and a pair of jeans over some flat boots, not very Brian-like at all. This merited investigation. As Brian admired Sophie's sensational horsebox, I whispered to Mum.

"I thought you'd be wearing something unsuitable, something Brian liked a woman to be seen in. What's going on?"

My mum turned a bit pink and faced me squarely. "I thought about what you said – about me doing what Brian wanted all the time. You were right. Brian was being manipulative. But I was to blame too, for letting him influence me."

I was a bit stunned. "Oh," I said. Not the most brilliant of responses.

"So I decided that instead of running away from the problem and simply finishing with him, I'd talk to him about it, put my point across."

"Oh," I said again. This was getting repetitive.

"He was actually quite sympathetic to my feelings and what I told him. I was surprised," said Mum.

She wasn't the only one – I almost fell over. At least I didn't say 'Oh' again. I was starting to get on my own nerves.

"So we'll see how we go. At least I didn't cut and run. We're working through it instead of just running away from the problem."

My mum had stood up for herself. That was great.

It meant Brian was still ongoing. That was bad.

"That's fantastic, Mum," I heard myself saying. "I want you to be happy."

"Where's Drummer?" said Mum, as Brian came over.

I took them to where Drummer was tied to the horsebox, munching on a haynet. He was thrilled to see Mum. "Here's a woman who knows about the important things in life!" he said, frisking her for sweets.

Mum dished out the Polos. Brian patted Drummer's nose.

"Is this the wally?" asked Drum, his minty breath wafting over us between crunches.

Mum wished me luck and assured me they'd both be watching us. Then, as it was time for James's jumping round and we were all getting a bit frantic and twitchy, she and Brian disappeared and left us to it. I didn't have time to think any more about my Mum and her new way of dealing with things, but I was certainly going to give it some more thought later when I didn't have such a hectic schedule because I was shocked, amazed and a little bit surprised.

Chapter Sixteen

We all helped James saddle Moth, tweaking her brushing boots, straightening her noseband and pushing James's tie right up to his shirt collar, then we followed them over to the show jumping ring. Everywhere was awash with Sublime Equine orange and lime banners, and the orange and lime dressed promo girls were there handing out catalogues and flicking back their hair. They looked just like Skinny Lynny. As all the dads ogled at them, the mums pulled disapproving faces and gave their husbands elbow nudges. Yup, just like Skinny, I thought with a sigh.

"The jumps look huge," gulped James, after walking the course and warming up over the practice fences. They did, but as Katy pointed out, in her official role of morale booster, that was because of all the fillers and flowers in them. They were, she assured James, no bigger than the ones he'd jumped at home.

James sidled up to me. "Can I borrow You-know-who for a quick confidence-building sesh?"

I screwed up my face. "Oh James, I can't. She's pinned into my pocket with like a million safety pins and it will take too long to get her out. Sorry."

James shortened his reins. "Well, we'll just have to do it on our own, won't we girl?" he said, patting Moth's chestnut neck.

Moth's bottom lip quivered and she looked straight ahead, all wide-eyed as usual, her white face making her look quite intense. If only she wasn't so nervous of everyone but James, I thought, stroking her neck. At least she'd stopped flinching every time I touched her. That was progress.

"You can do it, Moth. We all believe in you," I whispered. And then the announcer was telling the crowd that the next to jump was James Beecham and Gypsy Moth, and Katy, Bean and I held our breath and leant on the fence as our first team members cantered into the ring.

"Oh, come on James," said Katy, her fingers crossed.

The bell went and James and Moth raced through the start like they meant business, Moth's eyes open wide at the fillers and flowers. They flew over the first four jumps at a stonking pace and in great style and we allowed ourselves to breath out a little. Then there was a double, which Moth didn't like the look of – she snorted even more than usual, and James had to ride her strongly through, but nothing fell. A nasty, narrow gate was next, and although Moth's front hooves clipped it, it didn't fall (Bean put her hands over her eyes at this point and I think I actually stopped breathing), and they then raced over a wall, a hedge, a couple of big spreads and a water jump, before turning for the final three jumps, a nasty treble of shark's teeth.

"Come on . . . come on . . ." muttered Bean, jiggling up and down, riding Moth from the ground.

Moth took off too early over the first jump. Katy squeaked. Bean groaned and I dug my nails into my palms. Was this where our hopes fell apart?

The striding was all off for the second element, but Moth launched herself in the air and managed to clear it. But there was still the last jump to go. How could she do it? It looked impossible. Moth had no speed left and the last jump was a spread, needing to be tackled from a strong pace. We watched as James legged on, urging his gallant chestnut mare on with his hands and heels; we heard him ask her for an extra effort with a desperate HUP! and saw Moth take off way, way too soon. Surely disaster was inevitable?

I couldn't look.

Screwing my eyes shut I waited to hear the inevitable sound of planks falling, the groan of the crowd, the announcer shouting four faults. But instead, the longest ever silence was broken by the thud of hooves on grass, the crowd clapping, the announcer shouting *Clear Round*!

"YES!" shouted Bean, leaping up and punching the air.

"Oh brilliant, brilliant Moth!" screamed Katy.

"But how?" I said, astonished. "How?"

"She flicked her hind feet up over that last plank!" said Bean. "She's such a star!"

I'd missed Moth's Herculean effort by closing my eyes. I vowed never to be so wussy again.

Surrounding Moth as she came out, we all went a bit bonkers and told them how clever they both were.

"It was all Moth!" James said, sliding out of the saddle and giving his mare a big hug. "She was just the best."

And Moth actually looked pleased with herself. Instead of her usual shrinking, don't-look-at-me demeanour, her eyes sparkled as if to say, 'I did that, I pulled out all the stops and jumped my heart out for you all. I'm part of this team!' We each gave her a big kiss and a hug.

"What about me?" laughed James.

"We would if you were a horse!" laughed Bean, screwing up her nose and giving Moth another mint.

Talk about a missed opportunity!

Chapter Seventeen

Awaiting our turn in the collecting ring, I swallowed
hard. Drum and I really had to raise our game if we
weren't to disgrace ourselves in front of everyone. And
I had a score to settle with Cat – I just couldn't bear the
thought of her beating me, not after she'd tried to get
the Great Eight disqualified. My wimple wafted in
front of my eyes and I could hear a faint ting every time
Drum shook his head against a fly.

A boy on a black pony was performing his routine.
Dressed as a wizard, the boy rode his star-spangled
pony in ever-decreasing circles to a Harry Potter
soundtrack. Everyone around me murmured approval
and nodded their heads. He seemed to be the favourite
to win. I glanced around. Cat and Bambi had already
performed their routine and I could see them outside
the collecting ring with Leanne and Scott. I watched as

a woman joined them, a woman with a pushchair and two young children. Lifting the bigger child, the woman gaily plopped her on Bambi's broad back and I could see Cat looking less than happy about it. I was astonished – why was she was putting up with it? She wasn't usually so accommodating!

"How did Cat and Bambi do?" I asked Katy, watching the child drumming its feet on Bambi's sides.

"Er, I can just see the scoreboard," said Katy, standing on tip-toe and screwing up her eyes. "Pretty well, she's in the lead at the moment. She must be thrilled."

"She doesn't look very thrilled," I said, my heart sinking. "Who's that woman over there with her?" I asked. "She just plonked her child on Bambi – what a cheek – and Cat doesn't look too happy about it. Why doesn't she tell her to get lost? I would if someone did that to my pony!"

"That's just the problem . . . ," began Bean. "Ouch!"

I turned round and just caught Katy glaring at Bean, who was rubbing her elbow.

"What?" I said. "What's the problem? Who is she?"

"No idea," said Bean, a little too quickly. "Get ready, the wiz is almost done."

We were next – but I was determined to find out

what Katy and Bean were hiding. There was some big secret about Cat and Bambi, something the others weren't telling me. They'd refused to tell me what it was all about before. I'm still the new girl, I thought with a pang.

The star-spangled black pony came out hot and puffing. Taking a deep breath I glanced over at James who was in charge of my music. He gave me the thumbs up sign.

"Next to go is Pia Edwards and Drummer," announced the loudspeaker.

My mouth was dry and I could feel my legs shaking. My hand went to my pocket where Epona was safely stashed away. We needed some magic now.

"Come on then," cried Drummer confidently, jingling as he stepped forward, "let's knock 'em dead!"

His confidence rubbed off. It was now or never. Taking a deep breath, I stepped into the ring with him for our Hickstead debut – the stuff of dreams. Except that I didn't have a Union Jack on my jacket and I wasn't jumping for my country. I was dressed in a yellow frock and my pony wore bells on his ears. It wasn't quite a fulfilment of my lifetime ambition but hey, everyone has to start somewhere.

The ring seemed huge and there were what looked

like thousands of faces all turned in our direction. Strange then, that Catriona's face loomed out of the crowd, forcing my confidence into my boots. But then our music started and Drum was already into our routine. Tearing my gaze away from Catriona, I concentrated on the job in hand. I couldn't let Drum down now!

Drum was as good as his word – he was magnificent! He didn't just do the routine hoof-perfect, he jingled in all the right places, he tossed his head and gave exuberant leaps, he was just fantastic – talk about playing to the crowd! I remembered to smile and exaggerate my movements, and everyone loved us! They laughed in all the right places, and clapped like mad at the end. Except Cat, of course. She just stood outside the ring with her arms folded, looking sullen. Drum and I took a bow and skipped out of the ring where our team mates surrounded us.

"Awesome!" declared James, nodding his head.

"Oh, wow, well done Drummer!" cried Katy, dishing out the mints.

"You were so the best, Pia, by miles!" said Bean, even though she hadn't seen any of the others.

"Better than the Harry Potter wannabee, anyway," mumbled James.

We waited for the score. It was out of twenty, and anything over fifteen was considered pretty good. When it was written on the scoreboard I almost fell over.

"Oh Pia, you've got nineteen!" squealed Katy, dancing around in delight.

"You're IN THE LEAD!" screamed Bean, clutching my arm.

"Take that, Potter boy!" growled James.

I gave Drummer the biggest hug of his life. "You are the best pony in the whole world!" I told him, burying my face in his bobbly plaits.

"Yeah, yeah, tell me something I don't know!" said my pony. For once, I decided his smugness was justified.

There was no time to linger. Drum, Katy, Bean and I wandered back to the horsebox where Dee was getting ready for her showing class. I hardly recognised her. She wore a beautiful blue velvet cap on top of her hair, which was wound into a tight bun. With a cream shirt, blue and scarlet spotted tie, navy jacket, soft brown leather gloves, cream jodhpurs and brown boots, she looked a million miles from the scruffy Dee-Dee we were used to seeing at the yard.

"Wow, Dee, look at you!" exclaimed Bean.

"Yeah, I know, I look a right sight," Dee moaned.

"You look fabulous!" I said.

Dee's mum didn't think so.

"Dee, your tie isn't tight enough, and your hat's on wonky. Come here and hold Dolly . . . there. Oh for goodness' sake don't let her eat, she'll spit green slime all over herself. Must I do everything? Wake up! Stand still while I tie on your number. There. OK leg-up; one . . . two . . . no, are you doing this deliberately? On three, we always do it on three. Try again. One . . . two . . . three. Now ride her in over there – find a space – and get her on the bit and working properly. If she doesn't qualify for HOYS here then we might as well give up and take up knitting. And SMILE! Hello, hello?" Her mobile interrupted the tirade and instructions to Dee were reduced to hand signals and face-pulling.

Bean and I exchanged glances. If this was showing Sophie-style, no wonder Dee moaned so much. It was worse than being in the army. Dolly, however, seemed to love her showing career – from what I could hear as she trotted around.

"Tra-la-la . . . oh Crispin love, you look on fine form today. Is that Bilbo Baggins? My word, he's put on weight, far too much topline, whatever are they feeding him? Yoo-hoo, Lady Macbeth, you look wonderful darling. What is your human using on your coat? I can see my face in it!"

Sophie started up again: "Kick on, Dee, she's hardly moving. Get her going forward, she'll never catch the judge's eye like that! And SMILE, I said . . ."

"Crikey, Dee's mum's a total nightmare," I whispered to Bean. She raised her eyebrows and nodded, dumbly.

James came flying back, having been to look at the overall scoreboard. Breathless, he skidded to a halt, cannoning into Bean and knocking her flying.

"Sorry, Bean -- but hey, guys, I've got news. With a fast clear from Katy and Bluey, we'll be in the top five teams."

"We haven't gone clear yet," said Katy, unravelling Bluey's tail bandage to reveal his plaited tail. "And Bean's bound to do a fantastic test!" she added, kindly.

Bean shook her head. "You know I'm going to forget the test," she replied, "but at least my score can be discounted now you've all done so well. I just wish I didn't have to go at all."

"We'll be disqualified if you don't, remember?" I reminded her.

"That's right," agreed James. "But with Katy and Bluey as our sure thing and guaranteed a clear round, we're really in with a chance!"

Chapter Eighteen

It was time for our sure things to do their stuff.

"Does anyone know how that cheating Dweeb pony did in the jumping?" asked Bean, holding Katy's off-side stirrup as Katy swung herself into Bluey's saddle.

"Shhhh," said Katy, looking around to see if anyone had heard. "We can't say anything about that."

"She's last to jump," said James, grimly.

"OK, chaps," Katy said, patting Bluey's flecked neck. "Here we go. See you soon with good news, I hope."

Bluey was calmness personified as I heard Drummer and Tiffany wish him luck.

"Go eat up those jumps, you machine!" said Tiffany.

"Nothing less than a fast clear is acceptable," Drummer yelled as a parting shot.

I gave Katy the thumbs up sign. "Bluey's totally looking forward to it, no worries!" I told her.

Scott and Warrior were just finishing as we all got to the start of the cross-country. Warrior's breath came out in great puffs like a steam engine, and Scott looked cool, calm and collected. Catriona and Leanne were there, too.

"Another clear round!" Cat said to us.

"Congratulations, well done, Scott," James said.

"Yes, well done," I added.

'We don't cheat,' Cat mouthed to me.

I ignored my impulse to mouth back, 'Oh yes you do!' We couldn't say anything about the Dweeb and my conscience still bothered me. Was Cat right? Were we cheating? Was I cheating?

Katy and Bluey leapt over the first jump in a flash of purple and disappeared into the trees, out of sight. It would be some time before our team mates returned but the commentator kept us up to speed.

". . . and they're clear over the second and going nicely to the third. A good leap over the ski jump, and on to the next jump where they're clear again . . ."

It was all going well so far. James was right, they were a sure thing.

"Come on Bluey, do your stuff!" muttered Bean, her fingers crossed.

"Shhhh, listen," I said, "they're announcing the

results of Dee-Dee's class." The announcer from the showing rings boomed out over the loudspeaker.

First, Datchets Dolly Daydream, ridden by Delia Wiseman, second . . .

Whoever was second was drowned out by us all jumping up and down.

"YES!" shouted James. "This is *so* our day, we're all going home with Hickstead rosettes, yippee!"

"And she's qualified for HOYS," Bean pointed out.

"And the journey home with Sophie will be sweet. Imagine the atmosphere in the cab if Dee hadn't qualified!"

It didn't bear thinking about.

I suddenly became aware that the cross-country commentator was saying something I didn't want to hear. Something unbelievable.

". . . and they've jumped the wrong side of the flag – that's elimination."

"What's happened?" I cried. "They can't be talking about Katy, can they?"

The world seemed to stop as we all strained to hear the announcer. But we'd missed the drama, missed hearing exactly what had happened. Missed the moment it had all gone wrong for our sure things. Where did that leave the Great Eight?

Making our way to the finish, nobody dared to speak. I felt sick. Maybe we'd heard wrong, maybe the commentator had been mistaken. Bluey couldn't have gone wrong. Bluey never, ever went wrong.

Running back to the horsebox, we got there just as Katy and Bluey arrived back, too.

"What happened?" demanded James.

Katy looked totally crestfallen - and near to tears.

"I'm so, so sorry, it was all my fault," she said, closing her eyes at the terrible memory as she jumped to the ground.

I could hear Bluey whispering, "Sorry, I couldn't help it. I just couldn't help it."

"It was the jump coming out of the woods," puffed Katy, tearing off her hat and running her fingers through her hair. "The sun was shining brightly and after the darkness of the woods neither of us could see where we were going. The sun was blinding – I could barely see. It's moved round the sky from where it was this morning when I walked the course."

"I saw the jump at the last moment," moaned Bluey, distraught at his mistake. "I thought I jumped it, but I was the wrong side of the flag. I've let you all down."

"I messed up," continued Katy, unable to hear her pony. "The jump was narrow, it wasn't Bluey's fault. I couldn't believe it when I realised." She groaned, her shoulders sagging at the memory.

"Bluey's beside himself," I said, putting a supportive hand on Bluey's mane to show him we didn't blame him.

"Oh, Bluey, you couldn't help it," whispered Katy, kissing his cheek. "You're a star, you always will be."

"Yeah, Bluey, it's OK," said James.

"No-one blames you," said Bean. But she looked white because with Katy and Bluey out of the competition, Bean's dressage score had to count. It was the only thing standing between the Great Eight and disgrace.

Everybody knew it.

Nobody thought we stood a chance.

Chapter Nineteen

Katy was doing the maths – the trouble was, she was running out of fingers.

"We're not even in the running, now," she said, her eyes darting around the master scoreboard. "Because of me," she gulped.

"It was just one of those things, Katy. Don't dwell on it," said James.

"If India gets a fast clear with no time penalties, Team SLIC will beat us – we can't catch their score, even if Bean does remember her test," said Katy, grimly.

"See, even you know I'm going to forget it!" wailed Bean. There was ages to go before her time. Ages for her nerves to turn to quaking terror.

"No, I don't, honest," mumbled, Katy, fooling no-one. So much for her confidence-boosting talk.

"But if India gets a fence down, or goes too slow,"

continued James, studying the scoreboard intently, "and if Bean gets a fabulous dressage score" – he winked at Bean, who stuck her tongue out at him – "the Great Eight could still finish well up in the placings, beating Team SLIC."

Beating Leanne's team mattered to me – simply because I had an old score to settle. The Dweeb shouldn't have been competing at all. It wasn't a level playing field; India – whether intentionally or not – wasn't eligible to even compete. Somehow, beating Team SLIC was what mattered most.

"OK, let's go and watch India's round," said James. "However painful it is, I need to see it with my own eyes."

"We'll have to be sporting and congratulate them," sighed Katy. "If they do beat us," she added, glancing at Bean.

We all knew the chances of Bean getting a good dressage score were about a million-to-one. With Bluey's score discounted, our campaign was as good as over.

Why do we have to congratulate them? I thought. After all, they tried to get me disqualified. I didn't say anything out loud and remembered what my mum said about karma. But it was so hard, this karma thing! Katy was right, but knowing it didn't make it any easier. If we'd wanted to say something, we ought to have done so at the beginning, not now. We'd accepted the problem and run with it. It was too late to change our minds, that would just be spiteful. Bad karma – with knobs on. Suddenly, I could see in my mind the advert for the Sublime Equine Challenge and its description of the Wild Card event. *Anything goes!* it had said. Well, that could include a bit of pony whispering, couldn't it? It was all down to interpretation.

We got to the show jumping ring just in time; India and the Dweeb were already half-way round the course, the Dweeb's careful hooves clearing the poles and planks with ease, concentration showing on her rider's face as India steered her talented pony over the beautiful jumps. The rest of her team mates stood in a huddle, willing her to a fast and clear round. I couldn't believe India knew her pony's history. I just couldn't.

The Dweeb turned to the challenge of the final three jumps. They were nothing for an experienced pony and India galloped through the finish with a neat, fast, clear round, to the joy of her team, who went wild. India's delight shone on her face as she pulled up outside the ring, surrounded by Cat, Scott and Leanne, and her own mother, who had tears in her eyes.

"Oh India, you were wonderful!" gushed her

mother, dabbing her face with a tissue.

"No surprises there!" said James, grimly.

But he was wrong.

Suddenly, the party was interrupted by a blonde woman running up to the Dweeb. She patted the pony's damp neck as she drew breath.

"Platinum Bell!" she shrieked so loudly, everyone around the ring could hear. "I won everything on this wonderful pony — at the Horse of the Year Show and here at Hickstead. It's wonderful to see her again!"

India smiled and shook her head, "I'm sorry, but this isn't . . ." she began.

India's mother froze. Then she grabbed the woman's arm and tried to pull her away.

"You're mistaken. This pony's not called Platinum Bell," she said almost too loudly, too quickly.

"Oh, I'd know her anywhere!" the blonde woman laughed. "She's Bella all right — a bit older and her dapples have faded, but still the same. She was one of the most successful jumping ponies on the circuit!"

"What?" A formidable woman towing a Jack Russell on a lead rope her son was on another team — joined in. "This pony's an experienced jumper, did you say?"

"Only one of the most successful ever!" laughed the blonde woman.

"You don't know for sure," butted in India's mum. "You can't prove it."

"Well, she's still got the scar on her chest where she got caught up in the trailer one day," the woman said, pointing to a jagged black mark under the Dweeb's martingale strap.

We all looked at one another. The game was up. The colour drained from India's face as the full force of the woman's words hit home.

"That pony shouldn't be here!" the woman with the dog exclaimed, turning red with fury. Her son, on his dark bay cob, started whining that it wasn't fair and the Jack Russell, sensing an upset, bounced about on the end of the lead rope, barking.

"You don't know what you're talking about!" replied India's mum, jutting her chin upwards in defiance. But the large woman was having none of it.

"If that pony is who this woman says, she's too experienced for this competition. You're cheating and I'm going to lodge an objection and get you disqualified."

India's mum went scarlet. It was clear that she'd known all along about the real identity of the Dweeb. I glanced at Team SLIC. They all stood with their mouths open, amazed. No-one could doubt that it was a complete surprise to Scott, Cat and poor India.

Although James had already told Leanne, she was still horrified at the scene in front of her.

The crowd started whispering in excitement as the woman marched off on her mission to get India disqualified.

"Is this true, Mum?" India whispered.

"Well, India, I, er, I didn't know anything about this, er, honestly, love," her mum stammered. It was obvious she was lying.

"Oh Mum, how could you?" cried India, bursting into tears.

"Look, love, I just wanted you to do well. I just wanted success for you, for you to be happy. I wanted you to win. I did it for you . . ."

"God, this is just awful," I heard Bean whisper. "Poor India."

I felt sorry for her, too. It wasn't her fault. It didn't seem fair, somehow.

"So you cheated," yelled India. "And you made me cheat, too."

India's mum flinched like she'd been hit.

"And you made me let all my team mates down!" India continued, turning towards Team SLIC, who stood there silent and shocked, seeing all their hard work and dreams sliding away.

"But I did it because I love you, India, don't you understand?" her mum pleaded.

"That's too bad, because I hate you for it!" sobbed India, turning the Dweeb and cantering off across the showground.

For the second time that day I was grateful for my own parents. They're weird, but they'd never do anything like India's mum. She must have totally blown it with the karma thing. I thought I'd feel glad if India was found out but instead, I couldn't help feeling sorry for the disappointment the whole team was experiencing. In her effort to see her daughter succeed, India's mother had ruined any chance of success for the whole team. It was totally unfair, and our rivals didn't deserve it. I couldn't imagine how poor India must have been feeling right now. I didn't feel any better when Team SLIC's marks got wiped from the scoreboard. We'd been upset about them cheating, but when they were actually eliminated, we didn't feel victorious at all.

And then another, heart-stopping thought hit me: now that Cat was out of the competition, would she resurrect her campaign to get the Great Eight disqualified, too? Would she come gunning for me?

Chapter Twenty

"Are you OK, Bean?" asked Katy, as we all walked back to base. Bean nodded, robot-like. She looked ashen and anything but OK. We helped her get Tiffany ready. Actually, we got Tiffany ready – Bean couldn't do anything, she was in such a state. If Bean didn't compete, we'd be disqualified, and nobody wanted that. We'd come this far, we desperately wanted to finish. All the teams would parade in the main ring, and we didn't want to go home robbed of that chance.

Like Team SLIC had been, I couldn't help thinking.

Dee plaited Bean's hair and Sophie – all smiles now Dolly and Dee had qualified for HOYS – sprayed Tiffany with Dolly's very expensive show sheen, making her golden coat glimmer like a newly-minted pound coin.

"With any luck, the judges will be so dazzled by

Tiff's gleaming coat, they won't notice they're not actually doing the test," Sophie whispered.

As we walked over to the dressage arena, Bean's face turned even paler. Anxiously, I glanced at James and Katy who were keeping uncharacteristically quiet. They had to be sharing my negative feelings – and the India incident had left everyone feeling a bit wobbly. Swinging from Katy's hand like an instrument of torture was the noseband, ready to encase Tiff at the last moment. It seemed like the final insult – wearing a noseband for ritual humiliation in a test Bean couldn't remember.

"I'm going to let you all down," Bean whispered, shakily.

"No, you're not, Bean," I said, my heart pounding. I hoped my face didn't show my fears. "Just do your best. No-one's expecting any more than that."

Bean bit her lip and stayed silent in terror.

"You just have to do as much as you can remember, we don't want to be disqualified," said James, aiming a plastic smile at Bean.

If Bean was despondent, Tiffany was in a determined mood. I could hear her muttering to herself under her breath. "You can do this Tiff, noseband or no noseband. Come on, girl! This is the final time and you can do it, you can, you can . . ."

"It's time," James declared.

Bean looked at him like a condemned prisoner about to have her head cut off.

Katy fumbled with the noseband but this time, Tiffany didn't close her eyes. She took a deep breath and as their names were announced, the palomino trotted into the ring and around the outside of the dressage markers, waiting for the bell. I sidled up to James.

"Do you think Cat will try to get me disqualified again, too?" I asked him.

James's grinned. "There wouldn't be much point, now," he said, grimly. "It's not like we're in with a chance, is it?"

"But she still might," I said, chewing my nails. I didn't think Cat was the charitable sort.

The bell sounded and, miserably, we all leant on the rails. Would Bean remember the test? Even if she did, she couldn't possibly get a good enough score to make up for Katy and Bluey's shock elimination. Bean and Tiffany entered at C and rode straight up the centre line – but something was already wrong, Bean started to look wildly about her, as though she'd just woken up and hadn't a clue where she was.

"Oh no," wailed Katy, "she doesn't know where to go next."

"It's going to be a disaster," moaned Dee, her fist in her mouth.

"Come on Bean," whispered James, gripping the rails. "Come on."

But Bean sat like a dummy giving no signals to Tiffany, offering no suggestions of where to go.

Even though I had known, deep in my heart, that any chance the Great Eight had of doing well disappeared when Katy and Bluey jumped the wrong side of the flag, I had still allowed myself to believe that Bean might, against all the odds, remember this all-important, rehearsed-like-mad test.

Just this one test.

Just this once.

But now I knew I'd been kidding myself.

"She's forgotten the test!" I breathed. "She said she would and we didn't believe her. It's the end of the Great Eight's bid for glory!"

Chapter Twenty-one

The whole world seemed to slow down. Bean looked around frantically, obviously unable to remember where to go and what to do. Disqualification stared the Great Eight squarely in the face.

"Oh, I can't look!" moaned Katy, her head in her hands.

"We should never have made her do the dressage," sighed James – conveniently forgetting that he had been the one who had insisted on it.

"She told us she'd forget!" I muttered. "She told us all along!"

"Hold on . . ." Dee said, grabbing my sleeve, ". . . look!"

We all watched, breathless and open-mouthed as something amazing happened. Instead of a disaster, Bean and Tiffany had begun their test. Tiffany tiptupped around the corner in perfect rhythm and Bean suddenly sat up, quiet and still, looking more like a dressage rider with every step. They progressed with Tiffany on the bit, her paces even and with no sign of resistance, looking as though they competed in dressage every day of their lives.

"I told her she could do it!" said James, letting his breath out with a whoosh.

"She's fantastic!" whispered Katy, scared to say it any louder.

Even wearing the hateful noseband, Tiffany was doing a great job and Bean was like a rider possessed. It looked wonderful, Bean's blonde plait matching her pony's golden coat exactly, bouncing gently on the back of her navy jacket. Their transitions were bang on the letters, their turns and circles flowing and balanced, their paces regular. Tiffany didn't shake her head once. As they finished, we all let out a whoop of delight. It had been a fantastic test. In fact, I thought, it was as though Bean had been replaced by a Bean look-a-like who was fabulous at dressage. It was uncanny!

By the time we got to her outside the ring, the noseband lay in the grass and Bean was hugging her pony, tears streaming down her face.

"Tiffany, you're amazing!" she kept saying, hugging

Tiffany again and again.

"YOU were amazing!" shouted Dee.

"Bean, that was fantastic!" I said.

"Wow, Bean, you've been holding out on us. That was the best test ever!" cried James, shaking his head in disbelief.

"Way to go, Bean!" shouted Katy. "We told you you'd remember the test!"

"But I didn't," said Bean.

"You so did!" I yelled.

"No, it wasn't me. My mind went to mush as soon as I entered the arena," Bean said, wiping her eyes on her sleeves. "I just sat there, in a trance."

"But we saw you . . ." began Dee.

"It was Tiffany," explained Bean, hugging her pony again. "She did it all. She remembered the whole test. Thank goodness we practised it at home."

We all turned to Tiff, speechless.

"I promised I'd do my best," I heard Tiffany whisper.

"But it didn't look like Tiff was doing it at all," said Katy, astounded. "I mean, all the transitions were bang on the letters and everything."

"I know where to do it, give me some credit," snorted Tiffany. I told the others. We just couldn't believe it.

"That's got to be a good score," said James. He was all excited, looking towards the scoreboard.

"Oh, here comes the score now! I can't look!" muttered Katy as one of the Sublime Equine girls wrote Bean and Tiffany's score on the board.

"How much?" gasped Bean in disbelief.

We all stared at the board.

"Seventy-nine!" yelled Katy, jumping up in the air and letting out a whoop of delight. "You're so the dressage queen, Bean!"

"Bean, Bean, dressage queen," chanted Dee, thumping Bean on the back.

"Look out, Leanne, there's a new kid on the block!" said Katy.

"Oh Tiff, you are clever," Bean whispered to her pony, swinging off her neck in a bear hug.

"Careful," I heard Tiffany say, "I think that's a life-threatening object over there . . . and there's a funny noise around here . . . and I never EVER want to wear that hateful noseband again!"

And then I heard another voice I'd been dreading. It was anything but happy.

"You are such a cheat, Brighton. I'm going to see that your team is disqualified."

Catriona!

"Oh Cat, don't be like that," said James, in a soothing voice. "Getting us disqualified won't help your team."

"Please, Cat," said Bean, aghast, "how could you? We've always been friends, haven't we?"

"You wouldn't be so mean, surely?" added Katy.

"I don't see why you should be in this competition when we've been disqualified. You're cheating worse than us, with Brighton here being able to communicate with her pony in the Wild Card event," Cat said nastily.

"But you never believed I could talk to ponies!" I said.

"Yeah, well, it's not what I believe, is it? It's what the organisers believe!"

"Even if Pia can talk to the ponies," said Katy, carefully, "she can't make them perform any better, can she? You're being unreasonable, Cat. Pia's demonstrating her unique partnership skills with Drummer, just as the rules state she should."

"Come on, Cat," added James, winking at her, "be a sport!"

Cat's green eyes looked at James. "It isn't fair," she said. "You know it isn't. Why should she get away with it? Maybe you shouldn't have had her on your team!"

With that, Cat turned round and marched off in the direction of the secretary's tent.

"How can she be so vindictive?" asked Katy.

Our happiness had been short-lived. Now we were all plunged back into despair.

"She's not just hurting Pia, she's hurting all of us," said Bean. "We all used to be such good friends. I don't know why she's being so nasty.

Katy gave Bean a bit of a look. "It's not just because of India," she said. "She's upset because . . . oh, you know."

Bean nodded. "That's not our fault," she sighed. "She's taking it out on us."

"What are you not telling me?" I said, desperate to know the secret everyone but me seemed to know about Catriona. No-one answered.

"I'm going to talk to her . . ." said James, turning round and heading off after Cat. "See you back at the horsebox."

"What do you think he's going to do?" asked Dee.

"Kill her?" suggested Bean.

"If anyone can persuade Cat, James can," Katy said, thoughtfully.

I wondered what she could possibly mean. Could James save the Great Eight a second time? I felt terrible.

Everyone at the yard had been friends before I arrived. My pony-whispering had altered things. It was because of me that Bean was saying she would never see Cat in the same light again. Because of me, Katy said she would never have thought Cat capable of being so horrid. Because of me, James was going . . . to do what? Was Cat right? Was I cheating? I decided karma sucked.

Back at the horsebox, we waited around miserably for James to return. I didn't see how he could stop Cat from lodging an objection. Around us, the show went on – horses left the horsebox park for their classes, ponies returned with riders who were either euphoric or downcast, grooms rode in their charges.

Suddenly, James was back, breathless and red in the face from running.

"Get saddled up!" he shouted. "We're due in the ring any time now!"

"What?" We all gawped at him, unable to take in the significance of his words.

"Come on – we're still in the competition, and they're due to announce the winners at any moment!"

A wave of relief washed over me. James had done it – I didn't care how. Hastily, we bridled the ponies and Dee helped me into her showing outfit – I'd forgotten my jacket and hat, only packing my Wild Card get-up.

"But what about Cat?" asked Katy.

"It's all sorted," James said, dismissively, vaulting into Moth's saddle and cantering off in the direction of the main ring.

"Who cares about the whys and wherefores!" shouted Katy. "Let's go!"

Having abandoned the scoreboard in despair when Cat had appeared we had no idea where the Great Eight were placed. All the teams milled around the entrance to the main ring and the Sublime Equine promo girls were trying to put the teams in order, while the commentator was telling the crowd about the Sublime Equine big-wigs who were presenting the prizes. The Managing Director of Sublime Equine, a woman in a lime green suit and an expensive-looking hairdo, struggled on to the grass with a huge trophy.

"First place in the Sublime Equine Team Challenge goes to . . ." boomed the loudspeaker.

We knew it wasn't us. We'd worked that much out at the scoreboard.

"Team Stapleford Stables!"

Stapleford Stables were so good, three members of their team had won their events – pretty impressive and impossible to beat. They rode into the arena to thunderous applause.

"Which team are you?" asked a Sublime Equine promo girl.

"The Great Eight," Katy replied. "Have we come anywhere?"

The girl examined her clipboard. "Don't you know? Er, let me see. The Great Eight . . . can't see you on here . . ."

That doesn't sound promising, I thought with a sinking heart.

The loudspeaker drowned out the promo girl. "Second place goes to the Great Eight, James Beecham on Gypsy Moth, Charlotte Beanie on Tiffany's . . ."

The whole world seemed to stop. I looked at my fellow team mates and they looked back at me. I don't think any one of us had our mouths closed.

"Come on, hurry up!" said the Sublime Equine promo girl, shooing us along the famous Hickstead tunnel I'd seen on the TV, and into the ring.

Riding Drummer in the famous arena, flanked by James and Moth, Bean and Tiffany and Katy and Bluey, I knew what it felt like to win an Olympic medal – I couldn't have felt happier or more proud of our team. Everyone cheered and clapped. We heard our names over the loudspeaker and I thought this was the most amazing moment of my whole life. Drummer took it all in his stride, of course but Bluey felt like me, I could hear him being all proud and excited. We had to box Tiffany in because all the jumps and officials and photographers were making her freak. Moth was her usual, silent, trembley self.

We weren't quiet. We hugged each other, and pointed out people in the crowd – I could see Dad and Skinny Lynny actually in the tunnel (so I supposed wearing jodhpurs had its advantages – the organisers had obviously mistaken Lyn for a competitor!).

The rosettes were huge! We got two each – a second prize one, and an orange and lime finalist one. With one either side of his bridle, I could hear Drum moaning that he felt like a carthorse – blinkered.

But that wasn't all. After the team prize giving (we all won finalist vouchers for Sublime Equine outfits, plus a surprise £50 cheque each!), the announcer called out the winners of each individual event. I wasn't really listening – I was busy looking round to see if I could spot Mum in the crowd – so when James gave me a shove, I was just about to shove him back when I felt everyone looking in my direction. Something, it seemed, was expected of me.

"That's you!" hissed James.

"What is?" I said, being stupid.

"You've won the Wild Card event!" shouted Bean.

"You and Drum have prevented Team Stapleford Stables from cleaning up in every event!" James told me.

"Go on, go and get your prize!" said Katy.

I steered Drummer forward so that the Managing Director of Sublime Equine could present me with another huge rosette, a trophy and another cheque for £50. I couldn't believe it – especially when they got to the best bit, a fabulous blue Hickstead sash, which was like the holy grail to me. My face hurt, I was grinning so much.

When we all galloped around the vast arena on our lap of honour with the crowd's applause ringing in our ears, it was a moment I knew I'd remember for the rest of my life. And when Drummer put in a huge buck, I laughed and patted him in thanks for a job well done. My pony was such a star, and I was determined that he'd never feel unappreciated again. The Sublime Equine Challenge had been the most fantastic fun – but the fact that we'd learned more about our relationships with our ponies was worth more than the huge rosettes, more than the prize money, even my coveted sash – although they were fabulous, too! It was a fairytale ending to our Challenge – perhaps karma had worked for us after all.

Somewhere in the back of my mind was the niggling question of how James had persuaded Cat not to lodge an objection against me. I couldn't imagine what he could have said to stop her but right then I didn't care. Whatever he'd said, it was worth it, I thought. No-one could take away this fabulous feeling I was experiencing in the Hickstead main arena. I just wished I could have put out of my mind the image of poor India when she realised her dream had ended through no fault of her own, and the toe-curling feeling that the rift between myself and Cat had gone beyond any point of repair.

Chapter Twenty-two

"Thanks Drum, I love you so much!" I whispered into one of Drum's furry, black-tipped ears as we stood in the field at home.

"Mmmm," snorted Drummer, his black mane still curled and fluffy from the plaits, "I think I've had enough appreciation for one day. It's been death-by-hugging ever since we got those huge ribbon pizzas that pass for rosettes slapped on either side of me. I felt quite claustrophobic!"

"Oh, you loved it really!" I said, hugging him again. "And it's all over now."

"Does that mean I'll be treated with a bit more respect? I mean," he glared at me, "no more bells?"

I laughed. "OK, no more bells, I promise!"

Drum sank to his knees, sighing with the effort of rolling right over and getting both sides good and dusty. Rising with a grunt, a shake began at his head, rippling all the way through his body to his tail, the dust wafting off him in a cloud. I watched as he wandered over to the water trough for a long drink before settling down with the others in an all-night grass munching session. I had the best pony in the whole world – bar none.

Unpinning Epona from my pocket, I took her out and looked at her, rubbing the spot where her nose used to be.

"Thanks for your help, Epona," I whispered. Without her, I would never be able to hear Drum and the other ponies. She was worth all the trouble which always seemed to come with her.

Back at the yard, Bean was showing Mrs Collins her rosettes, Katy was mucking out her stable and James was lolling around on a bench outside the tackroom, stroking Swish. He seemed a bit quiet after all the highs and lows of the day.

"I suppose that's the end of the Great Eight," declared Katy, throwing dirty straw into the wheelbarrow.

"We were pretty great, after all!" mused James.

"The ponies were," I corrected him.

"Oh yes, the ponies were just brilliant!" agreed Bean, locking her tackbox. "Especially mine!"

Mrs Collins flip-flopped back to the house in her slippers, scooping up Twiddles-scissor-paws, all cute-puss with her, on the way.

"We have to take some of the credit, though," said Katy, shoving her fork into the barrow and pushing it out of her stable. "I mean, we overcame our problems, and our doubts and we did brilliantly."

"You mean you bullied us into it!" Bean reminded her.

"Yes, Katy, you'd make a fab sports coach," yawned James.

"That's right Katy, you have to take some credit, too," I said.

The sight of James yawning had made me suddenly very tired. We'd been up for hours and hours, and now the excitement had died down, I suddenly felt like I could sleep for a week. I felt deliriously happy and content – this was definitely going in my diary as one of my best-ever days. I couldn't wait to display my Hickstead sash in my bedroom, next to Drummer's rosettes. I still couldn't believe we'd won it. There was just one thing which had spoilt everyone's day.

"I still don't get it about the Dweeb," mused Bean.

I saw James roll his eyes. Unfortunately, so did Bean.

"Don't do that, James. How did India's mum pass

Platinum Bell off for the Dweeb? We all had to show our ponies' passports at Hickstead."

"She's right," said Katy.

I shrugged. "She must have forged the passport."

"Or Platinum Bell was passed off as another pony by India's mum before passports came into force," suggested James. "She's not exactly young."

"What's India's mum's age got to do with it?" asked Bean.

"No, Platinum Bell's not exactly young," I explained.

"Of course!" said Katy. "I bet India's mum wasn't the first person to profit from the deception – although she obviously knew about it."

"I still don't understand it," I said. "I know she wanted India to win, but what a dreadful way to do it! And do you know what?"

"What?" said Bean.

"I know it was unfair of Platinum Bell to be in the competition, but somehow it still feels unfair that poor India was disqualified – along with her whole team. I mean, she didn't know."

"I know what you mean," agreed Katy. "I wanted to beat Team SLIC fair and square, not have them taken out of the competition. It's awkward."

"And it's going to get worse, seeing Leanne and Cat

here every day," Bean pointed out.

"That's true," James agreed, stroking Swish behind his ear. Swish's hind leg thumped the ground – James obviously knew the exact spot to tickle.

"I still want to know what you said to Cat, James," said Katy.

"Don't ask," groaned James. "She was really upset – the whole team was crushed – you can't blame them."

"So what did you say to her?" asked Katy. She wasn't going to let it go.

"I just asked her," said James.

"Well we asked her. She didn't do it for us," said Bean.

James shrugged. He seemed suddenly very interested in Swish's collar. "I just asked her," he repeated quietly.

Suddenly, I didn't want to know how James had persuaded Cat.

"You asked her out!" Katy exploded, the words piercing my heart. "You know Cat fancies you!" Katy went on, her words digging deeper and deeper into my soul. "You did a deal!"

Bean stood open-mouthed, looking from Katy to James. There was no doubt that Katy had guessed the truth. James didn't deny it.

Because of me James was going out with Catriona.

Because of me . . .

"Shhhhh!" hissed James as Dee returned from turning Dolly out for the night.

"I told you, didn't I?" Dee said, oblivious to the atmosphere on the yard.

"Told us what?" said James, quickly, obviously relieved at the change of subject.

"I told you Granddad would help us. And he did!"

"Are you serious?" said Bean, astonished.

"Yeah, good old Granddad. I knew he'd come good. You have him to thank for your Hickstead success! Oh, and me, of course!"

Four of the Great Eight exchanged glances.

"Get her!" yelled James, leaping up and grabbing Dee, pinning her arms to her sides.

"Get off me!" Dee shrieked, kicking out as James lifted her clean off the ground.

Katy grabbed one leg, Bean the other and I helped James at the heavy end as we carried Dee, kicking and screaming, to the field.

"Whatever are you doing?" shouted Sophie, looking over Lester's half-door. Lester's liver chestnut ears were going like the clappers at the racket and he backed into his stable, snorting.

"Just going to dump her in the trough!" said James,

without breaking pace; like it was the most natural thing in the world.

"Oh," said Sophie. "Do it quickly, will you? You're upsetting Lester."

Dee's mum is so weird, you just never know which way she's going to go.

"NO!" screamed Dee. "I'm warning you, don't you dare, DARE, put me in the trough . . . Mum . . . HELP!"

"We'll teach you," muttered James.

"Yes, Dee, give the ponies some credit!" demanded Katy.

"And us!" added Bean, grimly hanging on to Dee's thrashing right leg.

"We," I said, as we dropped Dee into the water, "are the Great Eight! And don't you forget it!"

Dee gasped as she hit the cold water and she thrashed about, making herself even wetter. "I'm so going to get you all for this!" she spluttered furiously.

The ponies all lifted their heads and stared – except Tiffany: she took off down the field at a gallop, giving us a view of her tail.

"Oh that's nice," said Drummer. "How would you like us to come and dunk ourselves in your drinking water?"

"We'll clean it out," I assured him, a mass of emotions whirling around my head and my heart.

Because of me, Cat was James's girlfriend.

It seemed that Cat had her own victory, after all.

Out now: The Pony Whisperer

Runaway Rescue

Everyone at the stables is on alert when travellers return to the area. But Pia cannot help but be drawn to one traveller girl, Jazz, who has real pony-whispering powers. When she becomes a runaway, should Pia help Jazz — and risk her new friendships at the stables?